Ex-1

Laboratory assembly

JOURNEY INTO TERROR

BILL WALLACE

JOURNEY INTO TERROR

A MINSTREL® HARDCOVER
PUBLISHED BY POCKET BOOKS
New York London Toronto Sydney Tokyo Singapore

A MINSTREL HARDCOVER

 A Minstrel Book published by
POCKET BOOKS, a division of Simon & Schuster Inc.
1230 Avenue of the Americas, New York, NY 10020

Copyright © 1996 by Bill Wallace

Wallace, Bill, 1947–
   Journey into terror / Bill Wallace.
      p.   cm.
   Summary: A country kid and his half-brother from the city team up and learn from each other in order to save their lives in an adventure set in rural Oklahoma.
   ISBN: 0-671-00114-0
   [1. Brothers—Fiction.   2. Oklahoma—Fiction.   3. Adventure and adventurers—Fiction.]   I. Title.
PZ7.W15473Jo   1996
[Fic]—dc20   95-51028
                                                            CIP
                                                            AC

First Minstrel Books hardcover printing July 1996

10   9   8   7   6   5   4   3   2   1

*Dedicated to
Frank Hodge and the Hodge-Podge Bunch
Marianne Abbrat, Toni Scott and the Cy/Fair Kids
Peggy Charles and her kids in Skaneateles*

JOURNEY INTO TERROR

CHAPTER 1

Samuel? Please return to the house. We're going to be late," my stepdad yelled.

"Just a moment, Randall," I shouted back.

Justin Porter, my best friend, put a finger to his lips and shushed me. The morning air was so cold that his breath puffed out as a white cloud on either side of his finger. While I waited for Justin to unscrew the barrel of his BB gun, I pursed my lips and blew. Smoke swirled into the crisp Connecticut morning.

"You're going to love this, Samuel," Justin whispered. "I never knew a BB gun could do this until some kid at school told me about it. But it only works in the old models."

"The what?" I asked.

"The really old BB guns," Justin explained. "I mean, you try this with any other BB gun, one of the new air rifles, it jams in the barrel and you can never shoot it again. If the gun's just about old enough to throw away . . . well, those are the only ones that work."

"Right," I agreed, like I really cared. "Only in the old models."

The BBs made a rattling noise when he tilted the cylinder so they could roll out of the barrel.

Justin lived three houses down from us, closer to Norwalk. His dad was an accountant at some big firm in New York City, which sounded somewhat boring. But Justin told me that when his father was young, he was a sniper in Vietnam (wherever that was), and that he knew all there was to know about firearms. Each fall his dad took an elk-hunting trip to Montana, and he had promised Justin he could go when Justin turned fourteen.

I think Justin was eight years old when his dad told him. He talked his parents into a BB gun that Christmas and had been practicing every since. The lever-action air rifle was his constant companion. About the only time he left it home was when we went to school or to the mall in Stamford to play video games.

Once the BBs were out, Justin screwed the barrel back into his rifle. Then he reached down beside him and opened a box of kitchen matches. He cocked the lever, tilted the rifle upward and let one of the matches slide down the barrel.

"Watch this."

I propped my elbow on the birch log we were kneeling behind, and focused my eyes on the Coke can beside Mrs. Pipton's carriage house. Justin had shot twelve BBs at the can. It had eleven holes in it. He was quite proficient. I heard the puff of air as the spring expanded. Nothing happened.

"You missed."

Justin frowned.

"You didn't see it?"

"You missed the can," I repeated.

"I wasn't aiming at the can," he huffed rather indignantly. "Up there. On the wall of the carriage house. Here, I'll show you again."

He cocked the air rifle and slipped another match down the barrel. I watched the wall this time. The match hit the side of the carriage house, and there was a tiny but bright explosion as it struck. A yellow-blue flame and a little smoke swirled against the red paint. Then the match went out and dropped to the ground.

"That's something." He smiled. "Don't you agree?"

I shrugged. "Wouldn't it be easier to strike the match on the side of the box to light it?"

Justin rolled his eyes. "No," he scoffed. "This is like a grenade launcher."

"It's only a match and a BB gun." I shrugged.

"It is, but it works on the same principle as a grenade launcher. Well . . . it's smaller." He handed the air rifle to me. "Here, you try it."

I cocked the rifle and slid one of the matches into the upturned barrel. I aimed.

There was another flash of light and a tiny explosion. This time, the match stuck in the red paint that covered the old boards. It burned. It kept burning.

I felt the breath stop in my throat. In my mind's eye I suddenly saw Mrs. Pipton's carriage house bursting into flames. I was just about to put the rifle down and rush over there when the match went out.

"Man, that was a good one," Justin gasped. "What did you do?"

I shrugged and tried to return the rifle to him. He shook his head and pushed it back to me.

"No, do it again. Yours burned a lot longer than mine. I want to see what you're doing."

"It might ignite," I protested. "The carriage house might catch fire."

Justin shook his head and pointed at the barn. "The match was what burned. See? There's only a tiny black spot on the paint. Shoot another one."

I shot again. Then Justin took the air rifle and he shot, then he gave it back to me. We giggled, we oohed and aahed like people at a fireworks display when one of the matches would burn extra bright or extra long. It was kind of fun.

In fact, we were enjoying ourselves so much that we all but forgot the time. The once full box of kitchen matches was almost empty. There were only three left. Justin shot one then gave me the last two. I loaded the rifle. I aimed down the sights. I squeezed the—

"*Samuel William Ross!*"

The booming, unexpected voice behind me was so

loud, I jumped. When my finger jerked on the trigger—sure enough—I missed the whole barn.

Randall stood behind us with his arms folded. His forehead, which went clear back to the middle of his skull because of his receding hairline, was a bright red color.

"Samuel William Ross," he repeated. "What is the meaning of this?"

I shrugged and handed the BB gun back to Justin as if it were a molten piece of steel.

"We were just playing, Randall. We were just—"

He uncrossed his arms and jabbed an angry finger at Mrs. Pipton's carriage house.

"Look at that? Look at what you two boys have done!"

Sheepishly, Justin and I both looked where he pointed. There were about thirty matches dangling from the red paint. Justin leaped to his feet, ran to the building and started plucking matches out. I followed him.

"See, Mr. Brisk." Justin smiled as he stuffed the burned matches into his hip pocket. "See. It's good as new."

Randall didn't have his jacket on, but he still wore his vest and tie. (I think he even wore a vest and tie when he was mowing the lawn.) He crossed his arms over his vest and glared at us.

"There are burn marks—black carbon spots all over that wall."

"It's just a barn," Justin said, trying to defend us. "She'll never notice. She won't even—"

"It's not just an old barn," Randall growled. "It's an 1850s carriage house. Mrs. Pipton has restored it to its original form, and you two have defaced it." He brushed past us for a closer look.

"It will have to be refurbished," he said, his nose almost touching the barn. "I feel you two owe Mrs. Pipton an apology and she will deserve full restitution from your allowances. I suspect you should even provide the labor."

Justin leaned close to my ear. "How come your dad's got to use such big words? Why can't he just say, 'Tell Mrs. Pipton you're sorry, pay for the paint out of your allowance, and slop it on the barn?'"

I shrugged. "I guess because he's a lawyer."

Randall looked at his Rolex watch, then spun around to face me.

"We'll have to negotiate with Mrs. Pipton, but later, otherwise we shall miss your flight. Justin, go home and report this incident to your parents. Samuel!" He jabbed a stubby finger at our house. "Go! *Now!*"

CHAPTER 2

I watched in amazement as Mother raced through the house like a track star. She shouted at Randall to get his shaving kit from under the bathroom cabinet for me to use. She shouted at the maid to check the laundry for my blue Umbro soccer shorts. "Samuel, make sure you've packed your belt." She darted for the stairs. "Molly? Where are those Umbros?" When she raced back to my room to throw something else into my suitcase, she bumped into Randall. Both of them wedged in the open doorway for an instant. Mother pushed through first.

"We're going to miss your flight, Samuel. This packing should have been done last night. Where have you been?"

She didn't give me time to answer before she darted off again.

In a way, I was glad she was in such a panic. With all her running around and shouting, Randall didn't have time to tell her about Mrs. Pipton's carriage house. Maybe he'd have cooled off by the time I got back from Oklahoma.

Despite the fact that I was going to visit my real father for only two weeks, she had packed more than enough to last me for a month. I ended up with two bags. Each was so heavy that Randall had to carry them for me.

The taxi honked its horn. Mother held the door for Randall, and the three of us raced down the sidewalk. We'd just gotten in the cab when I remembered.

"My camera!"

I flung the door open and leaped out.

"Samuel? What—" Mother gasped from behind me.

"My camera," I called over my shoulder. "The one Daddy sent me for Christmas. He'd never forgive me if I didn't bring it."

I dug around in my sock drawer and found the camera, still in its case. The taxi horn sounded again. Feeling around deeper in the back, I finally located the two rolls of film I took last Christmas. The taxi honked a third time. Molly held the door wide for me as I bounded from the house and dove into the taxi.

It took us about twenty minutes to reach the airport at White Plains, New York. The second we arrived, Randall raced to the ticket counter to check my bags. Mother, still in a panic, grabbed me and headed for the gate. I'm glad she took hold of my arm, because if she'd had a grip on the camera strap around my neck she would have choked me.

She was in even more of a panic when we got to the security check and they wouldn't let us through because Randall had taken my ticket when he checked my luggage. Mother insisted that he was coming and that I was going to miss my flight to Chicago and the connection to Oklahoma City.

A man behind us in a business suit cleared his throat.

"Lady," he said. His breath smelled of cigarettes and alcohol. "The flight to Chicago has been delayed twenty minutes. They just now called for the pre-boarding passengers. You got plenty of time."

Mother thanked him, and for the first time in two hours she relaxed. I was glad. Mother was always so prompt and punctual that she managed to make me a nervous wreck every time we went someplace.

We moved to a little side corridor, away from the rush of people trying to get through the security check. She told me to wait there while she found Randall and my ticket. Although Randall had already assured her that since I was twelve I didn't have to wear one of those stupid tags around my neck and have a flight attendant seat me on the plane and drag me from one gate to the next, I was sure she would ask about that as well.

While I waited, I opened my camera case. When I looked at the exposure counter and saw that I'd only taken three pictures on that roll, the guilt swept over like a wave crashing on a beach.

My real father, whom I was flying out to visit in

Oklahoma, loved photography. He wasn't rich like my stepfather, and I knew the 35mm, single-lens reflex Canon with the zoom lens had cost him a bundle. The two rolls of film I had stuffed in my pocket were taken at Christmas, the day I opened the package. I hadn't even had the camera out of my dresser since then. It would break his heart if I had only two rolls of film for him to help me develop.

I popped the lens cap with my thumb and frantically began searching for something to photograph.

The side corridor where Mother had left me was virtually empty. People in the main corridor rushed by so quickly, I knew I couldn't get them in focus for a good picture. So, I looked out the window.

Outside, close to where I stood, were two Learjets on the tarmac. They were sleek-looking planes. Really neat. They sat facing each other with their pointed noses almost touching. I lifted the camera to my eye and brought them into focus.

Between the two planes some men stood, visiting. A man in a flat-topped straw hat and a man in a silly-looking brown derby were close together. The man in the brown derby was unrolling a large sheet of brown canvaslike material. It looked almost like a scroll. Five other men were clumped around them. I didn't really want the men in my shot. I just wanted the planes. But since there was no way I could scoot or tilt the camera to eliminate them, I went ahead and shot. I changed the lens setting and aimed again.

But just as I pushed the shutter button this time,

one of the men started jumping around. There was a sudden explosion of movement and I knew my picture was going to be blurred. I couldn't believe that the guy ruined my airplane shot.

Two of the men grabbed the guy with the straw hat and rushed him into one of the planes. Two others shoved the guy with the silly-looking brown derby toward the other jet. The man who had moved around and started the whole thing just stood there.

I looked at him through my camera.

He was a tall, slender man with dark skin. I twisted the focus wheel and tightened up on him with the zoom. I couldn't tell whether he was Spanish or Asian or maybe both. He had sunken cheeks and very smooth skin with no wrinkles at all. He was looking up, and even though I was a good twenty feet above him, he tilted his head way back. It was kind of like he was looking up—but looking down his nose at the same time. His eyes were what really caught my attention. He had tight eyes. They were so tight, they were like tiny slits in his head.

I lowered the camera and continued to look at him.

He was staring right at me.

I blinked, and when I opened my eyes again, he was gone. Frowning, I gazed out the window. The man was running toward the building.

"Samuel!"

Mother's voice startled me. I jumped. She grabbed my arm and nearly yanked me off my feet.

"Last call for your flight. Hurry!"

We raced through the security check and down the main corridor. At the gate she kissed me good-bye. Randall shook my hand.

"Remember," Mother said. "When you get to Chicago, if you can't find the plane to Oklahoma City, *ask!* Ask an airline official for help. And—"

The shrill sound of the metal detector at the security gate cut her off in the middle of her sentence. We glanced back. The man with the tight eyes was there, standing on tiptoes. He seemed to be searching the corridor. Then he put a hand under his left arm and backed up. When he was out of the detector, the shrill squealing stopped.

"And call us if you have any problems," Mother continued. "I mean, if there's anything you need, don't hesitate to call us. And have a good time with your father and his new family. And—"

An airline attendant stepped between us. "They're about to close the doors."

"And remember," Mother called as the attendant followed me down the ramp, "I love you."

CHAPTER 3

Once you've finished your tiny sack of peanuts and your glass of Evian water, there's not a whole lot to do on a long flight. I looked out the window for a while. Inside, I watched the businessmen in their dark suits and red ties. They weren't doing anything, either. Long flights were boring.

For a moment I thought about the guy with the weird eyes who came running through the airport, and how he had to stop when the metal detector screeched at him.

Maybe he was trying to catch the same plane I was on and his belt buckle or a cigarette lighter made him miss the flight. Man, I bet he was upset. Then I remembered how his tight eyes seemed to stare straight at me. But he couldn't have been looking at me, I argued with myself. I didn't even know the guy. So, I figured he had probably spotted Randall. Ever since my stepfather had entered the race for state senator, guys were always coming up to shake his hand or talk to him about politics.

I fluffed the tiny pillow under my head and nestled deeper into my seat.

As far as I was concerned, politics was as boring as long flights. I hoped things would be more exciting when I got to Daddy's. I closed my eyes and wiggled my head into the pillow.

Daddy had wanted to name me Sam Bass Ross. That's because his great-great-grandmother on his mother's side of the family was a second cousin, twice removed (or something like that) of the famous Texas outlaw, Sam Bass. Daddy, who was a western history buff, said that Sam Bass wasn't truly an outlaw. He was more like an "Old West Robin Hood"—a real hero type.

Daddy had told me he wanted the perfect name for his son. He'd said that he and Mother didn't have a name picked for me when I was born, but when he saw my steel-blue eyes, he knew. "The *best* of the Old West gunfighters had those steel-blue eyes," he'd told me time and again. "They were eyes that the other gunfighters feared. Men with those eyes never blinked, never flinched—they just drew and shot. That's why I named you after your great-great-grandmother's second cousin, Sam Bass."

Mother went along with the "Sam" part, only she changed it to Samuel because she felt Sam was too common and plain. The "Bass" part she changed to

William because "Bass" sounded like some sort of stinking fish. Besides, William was her father's name.

The "Ross" part was about the only thing they agreed on. It was about the only thing they *ever* agreed on. And even that didn't last.

Mother liked living in the city. Daddy loved the country. Mother enjoyed parties and crowds and shopping. Daddy liked being alone with nature. Mother appreciated central heating and air-conditioning and living close to museums and the opera. Daddy longed for an open fireplace with crackling logs and a rustic cabin in the woods.

Daddy worked as a photographer for a newspaper in Vermont. Every chance he got, he took off into the woods to photograph wildlife. Since I was so little back then, I spent most of my time with Mother. She worked for an interior decorating firm. We took a lot of trips to Albany or down to Long Island. We roamed the antique stores for furniture or found trinkets and craft items to put in other people's homes.

As opposite as my mother and father were, it was little wonder that they separated. In fact, I have a hard time imagining how they ever got together in the first place. At any rate, Mother and I moved back to Norwalk and Daddy stayed in Vermont. Like most little kids, I guess I blamed myself to some extent. Why—I don't know. I just imagine little kids do that. The guilt didn't last long, though.

Daddy caught the train and came to visit us almost every other weekend. He and Mother finally convinced me that I had nothing to do with their separation. Still, I kept hoping they would get back together. After eleven months their divorce was final and Daddy moved to Alaska. I had seen him only once since then. Only once in the past four years, and I couldn't help wondering . . .

The roar of the jet engines snapped me from my memories of Mother and Daddy. I sat up and tightened my seat belt. The tires squealed and I lurched forward as the jet engines reversed, slowing us on the runway.

Chicago's O'Hare Airport wasn't as bad as I had envisioned. I arrived at Gate K-11 and found out that my flight to Oklahoma City departed from very close by, Gate K-16. While I waited for the plane to board, I took pictures. The zoom lens was neat. I could focus on people who were waiting at other gates and they weren't even aware I was watching them.

I still had three exposures left when they called us to board the plane for Oklahoma City. I really wanted to finish off this roll and load a new one. Daddy would be disappointed that I had only shot three rolls. Still, three rolls were better than two. Maybe when I landed . . .

The plane was smaller than the one from White Plains, and I had a row of three seats all to myself. Guess not that many people wanted to go to Oklahoma. I stretched out on the seats and nestled into my pillow.

*   *   *

Daddy had loved the Alaska wilderness, but he'd hated the cold and snow. When he moved back, two years ago, he came for a visit. He took me to the zoo and we spent a long time talking—trying to get reacquainted. When he left, he told Mother and me that he'd met a young lady in Alaska. They were moving to Oklahoma, where she had lived before, and they were to be married in the spring. Mother seemed happy for him. Three months later she married Randall.

The summer before last, Daddy wanted me to come for a visit, but the move from Alaska had left him rather short of money. Last summer he wanted me to come again, but he was just starting a photography business to support his new wife and her son, a boy about my age. So once again he couldn't afford my ticket.

Now—with the exception of a quick trip to the zoo—now, after not really being with my father for four years, I was about to join him in Oklahoma for two whole weeks.

I sat up. I pressed my cheek against the window. It felt cold on my skin. Then a chill came, not from my cheek, but from deep inside.

Why was I going to Oklahoma? Randall called it a "fly-by," which meant it was one of those states you flew over on the way from the East Coast to California—but never visited. What if it was still a dust bowl? What if there was nothing there but dust and Indians?

The land below was squared off into plots—farmland. From 26,000 feet it seemed as flat and empty as our living room carpet. What if Oklahoma was flat and empty?

I swallowed the tiny lump in my throat. What if there were no shopping malls with video-game rooms? What if there were no soccer fields? I'd be stuck in a dust bowl for two weeks with nothing to do.

I didn't even know my daddy—not anymore. What if his new family didn't like me? What if they hated me? What if Daddy loved his new son more than me? What if he didn't want me anymore?

CHAPTER 4

Daddy was still my daddy.

When I first saw him, I could tell. I was about half-way back in the line of people who streamed up the gateway toward the terminal. There was a group just outside the doorway, and beyond them I could see my daddy. He kept jumping, trying to see over the crowd to find me.

He looked like a kangaroo, hopping up and down. When he spotted me, his face lit up like a Christmas tree. He forced his way through the crowd, swooped me up in his arms and hugged me until I felt like my eyes were going to bug out. Finally he put me down and led the way toward the baggage claim area. Every five or six steps, as we walked, he reached over and hugged my shoulders or patted me on the back to tell me how happy he was to see me.

"You brought your camera. That's great. I'm glad you like it. We've got a darkroom at home. You and

I can develop *all* the film you brought." He ruffled my hair. "I can hardly wait for you to meet Gary. You two are gonna hit it off great. I can tell. Patricia's sweet, too. I think you'll like her. We're gonna have a fantastic two weeks."

The Oklahoma City airport was about the same size as White Plains. Only the Oklahoma City airport seemed totally deserted. There were hardly any people at all. It didn't take long to get my suitcases and find Daddy's car. Well, it wasn't a car. It was a pickup truck. The thing was old and ragged looking—nothing at all like Randall's Ferrari. Daddy tossed my bags in the back and hopped in the cab. The thing was so high off the ground, I had to climb to get into it. The old truck rattled, squeaked, and bumped even on the smooth pavement at the airport. My back was a bit tight from all the flying I had done, and I seemed to notice every little jar and bounce.

Daddy turned right at the edge of the airport, then right at a stoplight. I could see the airport on one side. On the other there was nothing but pasture, a few trees, and some horses. There were no houses, and the road was narrow and bumpy. Ahead of us I could see where the pavement and the road turned into gravel.

It made me a little nervous. I knew that Oklahoma wouldn't be as "civilized" as Connecticut, but I had at least expected the state capital to have paved roads.

I mentioned something about how I thought Oklahoma City was bigger. Daddy explained that he was taking kind of a shortcut to avoid the traffic and that most of the city was behind us. He turned left before we reached the gravel portion of the road. I was glad. We drove a little ways and stopped at a convenience store.

"Always got to hit the Love's store before I head home." The door squeaked when he opened it. "Gas is always cheaper here than at Lawton. Got to get me some coffee, too. You want a Coke or somethin'?'

I shook my head.

"I don't drink carbonated water. Just a little Evian."

Daddy frowned. "What's that?"

"Bottled water."

"Oh," he said, then he shrugged and started putting gas into the old truck. "Might as well come in with me. Wouldn't even know where to look for that Evian stuff."

I was afraid that Oklahoma would be as backward and desolate as Randall and Mother had led me to believe. But inside the store I found my Evian. Maybe there was hope after all. We left the Love's store and pulled onto a nice four-lane highway.

"How many towns do we have to go through before we arrive?"

Daddy scrunched his mouth up on one side. "Let's see. There's Chickasha. Only we'll be on the toll road so we really don't go through it—just past the east edge."

"What did you say? Chick-a-what?"

"Chickasha," Daddy repeated. "It's an Indian

name. Sounds sort of like Chickasaw. You know, the Indian tribe? Only with a long A on the end. Anyway, we pass it, then we get off at Elgin and have to go through Porter Hill. That's three."

Only three towns, I thought with a smile. With luck, we would be at Daddy's in twenty minutes or so.

It didn't take long to figure out that towns in Oklahoma weren't like towns on Long Island. We drove and drove and drove. There was nothing on either side of the road. Nothing but rolling hills and trees. Every now and then I'd see a house and some cows or horses, but no towns. Along the southeastern coast of Connecticut, the towns were pretty close together. The houses were sprinkled out along the road, so sometimes I never knew when we left one town and entered another.

Out here, it took us almost an hour before we reached the town with the funny-sounding Indian name. No wonder Randall called Oklahoma "the wide-open spaces." There was nothing here but empty land.

After Chickasha, things got worse.

The houses were farther and farther apart. The ground seemed to flatten out. It was mostly grass, and the only place I saw trees was along the creeks.

Daddy kept trying to make "small talk." He asked about Mother and how I liked Randall. He told me about his new wife and son. Then he asked about the sort of things I enjoyed doing. I told him about soccer and playing video games at the game room in the mall or on my home computer. His only response was:

"You might find things a little different here."

After another hour we left the four-lane at a little town called Elgin. In the distance, Daddy pointed out some bluish-colored humps that rose above the flat land.

"Those are the Wichita Mountains," he announced proudly.

"Mountains?" I said, not quite believing the lumps could be called hills, much less mountains. "Those are mountains?"

"Well," he admitted, "they're not very tall compared to the Rockies or even the Catskills, but they're mountains. It's one of the oldest mountain ranges in the world. Once we get into them, I think you'll be as fascinated with them as I am. They're really extraordinary. Our house is nestled right against them. We're not very far from the Wildlife Refuge fence."

We turned left at Porter Hill. There were two gas stations, two stores, and six houses. That was all. I didn't know how they could get by with calling the place a town. We stayed on the highway for a while, then we turned right. The road was narrow and didn't even have yellow and white lines on it. Then we turned on another road that was nothing but gravel, and from there onto a dirt road, and from the dirty, dusty road onto something that looked like two parallel paths with grass growing between them.

Any moment I expected him to stop the pickup beside two saddled horses. We'd have to ride, then as the terrain became worse, we'd be forced to abandon the horses and walk. Finally we'd have to swing by vines to reach Daddy's house.

When the truck bounced and rattled through the bottom of a dry creek bed, Daddy pointed to a wood-frame house atop a hill.

"There's the house." Daddy smiled proudly. "We're almost home."

I tried to hide my disgust behind a fake smile. I couldn't believe we were so far from civilization. There were no towns, no shopping malls. Nothing. As we neared the house, I cringed.

The hill where it sat probably wasn't the "End of the World"—but I bet I could see it from there.

CHAPTER 5

*F*rom the dry creek bed the house looked like it was rotting and about to fall down. As we drew near, I realized it was made of rough cedar. A few of the finer condos and cabins around the Finger Lakes, especially near Skaneateles, where we summered in New York sometimes, were made of the same material. It gave the place a rustic look. The house had a big front porch. Six huge cedar logs supported the overhang from the roof.

Daddy turned the motor off, honked the horn, and hopped out. I opened my door, but I didn't hop out. My legs were weak. I hurt all over. So I more or less oozed from the truck—one leg at a time—so I wouldn't fall.

A woman opened the front door and stepped onto the porch. She had short brown hair and a pretty smile. She looked a lot younger than Mother. At first glance I thought she was a bit plump. But when

Daddy got my suitcases and leaped up on the front porch to give her a kiss, she turned to kiss him back. When she turned sideways, I realized she wasn't plump at all. She was really quite slender—slender, everywhere except her tummy. It pouched way out like she had a soccer ball hidden under her dress.

My new stepmother was going to have a baby.

"Sam." Daddy waved for me to follow. "Come on up here and meet Pat."

I just stood there, staring at them. I didn't know why. I didn't know how I felt.

My daddy and some woman I didn't even know were going to have a baby. And somehow, it was going to be related to me. If Daddy had warned me . . . if he'd said something on the phone when we were planning the trip . . . maybe it wouldn't have been such a shock and . . .

"Come on, Sam." Daddy motioned again.

My legs were stiff, but I started toward the porch.

Was I supposed to be happy? Was I supposed to be mad because my daddy loved some other woman besides my mother? I didn't know what to do or how to feel. All I could do was stagger to the porch and stand, gaping at the lady's round tummy.

"Patricia, this is my son, Sam," Daddy said. "Sam, this is my wife, your stepmother, Patricia."

I saw a hand. I took it and shook politely, only I didn't look up. I guess I was staring so hard, I didn't even realize I *was* staring. Not until Daddy put a hand on my shoulder.

"You're going to have a new baby sister."

I jerked my eyes away from the woman's stomach and focused on him. Daddy's chest was puffed out and his smile was proud. He shrugged.

"Well, the doctor did an ultrasound and said it was a girl. But who knows. Anyway, she's due in about two months. Isn't that somethin'? You're gonna have a sister. Well, a half sister. What do you think?"

I didn't know what I thought. So I just smiled up at him and nodded. His smile broadened. He slapped me on the back, then turned to the woman again.

"Where's Gary? I can hardly wait for these two guys to get together."

Patricia gave a slight tilt of her head.

"He's back by the barn trying to figure out what to do with that soccer ball you bought." Her voice was soft and I heard an easy southern drawl that made her words flow like the little stream behind Justin Porter's house.

Daddy put my bag down and trotted to the edge of the porch. He took a deep breath, pressed his little fingers against the corners of his mouth and blew. A high, shrill whistle pierced the still air. It was so loud, it made me cringe.

"Gary, come on to the house. Sam's here."

I felt a gentle hand on my arm. I looked up. Patricia's smile was as soft as her touch.

"I asked your father to tell you about the new

baby," she said. "He wanted to surprise you. I'm sorry it was *such* a surprise."

"Oh, it's all right," I lied. "I think . . . it's . . . ah . . . well, I think it's wonderful. I'm most happy for the both of you."

When she looked away, I felt my eyes roll in my head. I didn't know what I was saying. The words that came tumbling out had sounded like some of the polite conversation Mother made at one of her club meetings. I hoped I didn't sound like a total idiot. I hoped it was the appropriate response.

"Gary?" Daddy yelled again.

"Coming, Dad," a faraway voice called. "Stupid ball went and rolled off the cliff again. Had to go fetch it."

I felt my nose crinkle. ". . . ball *went and* rolled off the cliff? . . . *go fetch it?*" What kind of ignorant hick could possibly talk like that?

A boy appeared at the far side of the porch. He had a soccer ball tucked under his arm like a football. About my height, he was dressed in faded denim blue jeans and a dirty white T-shirt. He put his free hand on the porch rail and hopped over. As he trotted toward me, I offered him my hand.

"You must be Gary," I greeted. "I'm Samuel."

Only, instead of shaking hands with me, the kid tossed me the ball. It startled me, but somehow I managed to catch the thing. He trotted right past me.

"Come on, Sammy," he called, reaching for a suitcase. "I'll show you our room, then we can—" A sudden pained grunt cut his sentence short when he lifted my bag. "Dang! What y'all got in here, barbells or somethin'?" Straining, he had to lean to the side to get the suitcase off the ground. "You into weightliftin' or stuff like that?"

I shook my head. "No, it's just my clothing and—"

"Clothes!" he yelped. "Man, you're only stayin' a couple of weeks. Feels like you packed for a whole year. Grab that other'n and c'mon."

I stood there with my mouth gaping so wide, I could have put the soccer ball inside and never felt it.

The kid called me "Sammy!" I hated *Sammy!* He didn't know how to greet someone properly. He didn't shake hands. On top of all that, he talked like he was from another planet or something. "Dang . . . y'all . . . fetch it . . . grab that other'n . . ." I shook my head. My mouth made a popping sound when I forced it shut.

Daddy picked up my other suitcase and put the handle in my palm. He closed my fingers around it.

"Go on upstairs and unpack," he said. "I have to go get the charcoal started. Thought I'd broil us some buffalo burgers for supper."

My knees felt weak. My eyes seemed to swirl and throb in their sockets. I just knew I was going to pass out.

Here I was, stuck in the backwoods of Oklahoma, miles from any form of civilization. Stranded here for two weeks with a pregnant lady and a "companion" who had no manners whatsoever. Deserted, for an eternity, with some hick moron who called me *Sammy* and who couldn't even speak English. And now . . .

now, my own father was going to poison me by feeding me . . . What did he say?

Buffalo burgers?

My only thought as I staggered up the wooden staircase was:

I WANT TO GO HOME!

CHAPTER 6

I want to go home!"

"Now, Samuel," Mother's voice came soft yet stern through the telephone receiver. "You know your father's been planning this visit for two years. You just arrived last night. Give it a day or two. I'm sure that if you would simply—"

"I want to go home!" I repeated, cutting her off. I heard Randall pick up the extension phone. I kept on talking. "You don't understand, Mother. They made me eat bison. The boy—this Gary person—he has no manners. He's totally uncivilized. He talks funny and he even ridiculed my clothing."

"Why?"

"Well," I said, frowning at the telephone, "he inquired as to what I was doing with . . . how did he phrase it . . . 'all them Sunday-go-to-meetin' clothes.' He also informed me that I would probably 'bust my butt with *them thar* slick shoes.' "

Mother sighed.

"Well, perhaps I should have sent you a few more casual outfits. I thought about your tennis shoes but I was reluctant to put them in your suitcase because of the aroma. Perhaps you could run to the mall and—"

"There *is* no mall," I yelped. "We are in the backwoods. It's a half-day pilgrimage just to reach a paved road."

"Now, Samuel"—Randall cut in—"that sounds like a slight exaggeration. From your father's description of his location, you're not far from that lake. The lake is near Lawton, which is supposed to be the third largest city in Oklahoma. Surely there are suburbs and small communities surrounding the lake, and—"

"No, Randall. This place isn't at all like the Northeast. The towns are hardly populated enough to be called towns, and there is absolutely nothing in between them. We're two miles from the lake, and this side of it is adjacent to what they call the Wildlife Refuge. It's like a national park or something. There *are* no houses nestled around the lake, like up in Skaneateles. There's nothing but wilderness. We're miles from the nearest house and—"

"Now, Samuel"—Randall's voice was gruff—"calm yourself. You're becoming hysterical."

I didn't realize I was shouting. Not until Randall shushed me. I cupped my hand over the telephone. The others in the house were still asleep. I didn't want to wake them. I leaned over, pressing my forehead against the kitchen wall, and humped my shoulders as if trying to hide the telephone and the sound of my voice deep in the curve of my body.

I hadn't been able to sleep, so I'd gotten out of the bed long before sunrise. In the dim twilight of morning, I had peeked out the windows at the empty wilderness surrounding the house. I sat at the kitchen table and waited until seven o'clock—that would make it eight back home—then I had called for help.

"Please come after me," I begged. "I can't stand it here."

"Now, Samuel," Mother soothed.

"Please! It's terrible. Horrid. They eat with their elbows on the table. Gary belches and eats with his fingers. He sleeps on a cot near my bed and flounces around and makes weird noises *all night long.* He doesn't even bathe or brush his teeth before he goes to sleep. He sits on the edge of the bed and cleans his fingernails with a pocketknife. And . . . and he even digs at the toe jam between his toes with his dirty socks instead of a washrag. Please. I want to go home."

"Sam, is that your mother?"

The sound of Daddy's voice startled me. I jumped. My head bumped the kitchen wall, where I leaned against it. Somehow I managed to catch the phone before it hit the linoleum.

Daddy stood behind me. I could tell from the hurt look on his face that he'd overheard at least part of my conversation with Mother. I didn't intend to wake him. I felt really rotten that he'd heard what I'd said about Gary and about them eating with their elbows on the table. As I looked at his sad, hurt expression, guilt swallowed me like a fog that sweeps in from the ocean.

Daddy reached out.

"May I speak with her, please?"

Sheepishly, I handed him the telephone.

"Samantha, this is Tom . . . Yes, I'm fine . . . He's fine, too—at least physically . . . No, Randall. I don't think it's jet lag. It's more what I'd call culture shock."

I could only hear Daddy's part of the conversation. I listened intently, trying to guess what Mother and Randall were saying.

"Well, I'm sure he's exhausted from the flight," Daddy continued. "I doubt that he got much sleep . . . No, we got to bed early, but you know, having to share a room with a complete stranger and the unusual surroundings . . . Yes, I'm sure that has a lot to do with it . . . Yes, that too. But things are simply different here than in Connecticut . . . Yeah, Gary's a good kid. Really. He's just quite a bit different from the kind of people Sam's used to. He's never been to a private school or taken instruction in etiquette or . . ."

They talked for what seemed like hours. At times Daddy seemed to be defending his new family. I felt badly about putting him in that position. I didn't mean for him to catch me on the phone. I just wanted to go home.

From the conversation, at least Daddy's part of it,

I found out that he planned to crowd all his photography sessions into this week so he could take next week off to spend with me. He told them that the drive to Lawton was a good forty-five minutes, and since his old truck used so much gas, he usually made only one trip in and one back per day. However, since I needed some jeans and tennis shoes, he'd take the whole family with him today. "Patricia has a doctor's appointment tomorrow," he'd said. "We had planned to take the boys to town then. But we can go today instead and hit the mall." (I couldn't believe Lawton really had a shopping mall.) "I'm sure the boys can find some way to entertain themselves tomorrow while she's at the doctor's."

He also explained that as far as taste, bison was quite similar to hamburger, but it was a great deal lower in fat and cholesterol. "Sure. If we can find some way to pack it in dry ice," he'd told them, "I'd be happy to ship some back with Sam when he returns home."

He kept assuring Mother and Randall that I was fine. I think he was reassuring me as well because as he talked he kept looking at me. As the conversation drew to a close, they agreed that I should wait a few more days before deciding whether or not to go. Daddy said he would have me call them on Saturday to let them know how I was doing. He was just about to hang up when his face suddenly brightened.

"Really!" He almost laughed. "No. Nobody called last night. They'll probably call today . . . Yeah, if we're in town, the answering machine will get the message . . . Yes. It's fantastic . . . Darned right, I'm proud of him . . . Of course, I'll be sure and tell him . . . Right. I'll have him call you Saturday. Good-bye."

Daddy hung up the receiver and smiled at me.

"You get all that?"

"Yes, sir." I nodded. "Most of it, except for the last part. Somebody's going to call me?"

" 'Morning," Patricia greeted from behind us. She plodded into the kitchen in a red bathrobe and slippers. "You two are up early. Reckon I better get breakfast started."

"Pat, you're not gonna believe the news I just got from Samantha." Daddy bounded over to her and wrapped his arms around her. He picked Patricia up and spun her around. They both laughed.

"Well, what's the news?" she asked when he set her down.

Daddy pointed at me. "Randall just told me that a man called them last night from Placerville Photography Studios." He strutted over to me and put a hand on my shoulder. "One of the pictures that Sam submitted for their contest has just won second prize! Can you beat that?" He ruffled my hair, then started tickling me. I squirmed, trying to get away from his fingers. "That's my boy! A real photographer, just like his old man." He laughed.

He took my hand and started shaking it. He shook it so hard and for so long, my arm felt like a strand of limp spaghetti.

"I'm sure proud of you, son. Real proud! What was it, landscape? Portrait? Still life?"

Daddy's smile stretched clear across his face. The tiny wrinkles that surrounded his eyes seemed to tug at and wiggle his ears. I'd never seen him look so happy. I had hurt his feelings by calling Mother to come and rescue me. I made him feel bad by talking about how they ate with their elbows on the table and how I felt about Gary. But now all that was forgotten because he was so happy about my winning second prize in a photography contest. As I looked at his smile, as I saw how the pride puffed his chest out . . .

I just didn't have the heart to tell him it was some kind of mistake. I didn't have the courage to tell him that I had never entered a photography contest and that I'd only shot three rolls of film on the camera he sent me last Christmas. So . . .

"A portrait," I lied. "A picture of Mother."

CHAPTER 7

It was weird.

Second prize for photography? *Me?*

I felt guilty about lying to Daddy. Patricia began preparing breakfast. Daddy put some coffee in the percolator. The photography thing was probably some kind of sales gimmick or promotional scam. Still, Daddy had been so happy. I felt even more guilty about lying to him. I was just about to confess when Gary came into the kitchen.

He was dressed in nothing but his Jockey shorts. He scratched his bottom and yawned about three times without covering his mouth.

" 'Mornin'," he greeted us. "Reckon we might get in a little fishin' after breakfast, or'd you rather play some of that soccer stuff?"

"You'll have to save the fishing or soccer until this afternoon," Daddy answered for me. "This morning you and Mom will run me in to the shop, then take

Sam to get some jeans and stuff at the mall. You boys can play after you get home."

Then he told Gary about the photography contest I had won and we sat down to eat pancakes. Patricia's pancakes were better than the ones Molly prepared back home. I ate four of them and felt like I was about to explode when I finished. Daddy went upstairs with us to dress to go to town.

"Let's see what all you have in those suitcases," he said, sitting on the side of the bed. "Might need more than a pair of jeans and a pair of tennis shoes."

I opened one suitcase and handed him the packing slip Mother had enclosed. Daddy smiled.

"Samantha always was one for organization. Let's see what she's got in here. Three pair dress slacks. Three white shirts, three ties. One black suit. One navy-blue blazer. Fleece-lined jacket, socks, underwear, two toothbrushes . . ." He kept reading, only instead of reading out loud, he read to himself. His lips kept moving, though. Finally he concluded with, "Six Izod knit polo shirts and six pair of casual slacks."

"See," Gary called from inside his closet. "Just like I told you, Dad. Sunday-go-to-meeting clothes."

Daddy looked up at me and smiled. I smiled back at him and tried to ignore Gary.

"She did pack six casual outfits and my old shoes."

Daddy sighed and laid the list beside him on the bed. "Sam, casual in Norwalk, Connecticut, and casual around here are two different things. What you have is okay for playing volleyball in someone's backyard or walking to the mall. But in this area, with the terrain we have—"

"Yeah," Gary interrupted. He hopped out of the closet on one foot while pulling up his pants. "If you wear slacks in the briars we got 'round here, they'd be eat up in thirty minutes."

"And as far as the shoes—" Daddy started.

"Yeah," Gary broke in again. "We go up in the mountains and old Sammy and his slick leather-soled shoes are gonna spent more time on his butt than exploring." He turned to me and zipped his jeans. "Sammy, I figure you're gonna need at least three pair of jeans and two pair of tennies."

"Why two?" Daddy asked.

"Sand bass are fixin' to start running up to the head waters of Lake Lawtonka. They start bitin', even I get excited and end up in the water, sometimes. You can imagine what some city kid's gonna do."

I forced the sneer from my face and got an outfit out of my suitcase to wear to the mall. *City kid* . . . *Sammy* . . . Man, this guy was sure pushing his luck. If Daddy wasn't around, I'd . . .

"Okay." Daddy got up from the bed. "Find him three pair of jeans and some T-shirts. No sense messing up his nice clothes. I'll tell Mom to get two pair of tennis shoes."

"Better make 'em high-tops," Gary called as Daddy went to get dressed. "Reckon his ankles ain't used to all the rocks. High-tops will give him a little more support. Keep him from falling down so much."

Falling down, indeed, I seethed in my silent anger. Called me Sammy. Talked about me like I wasn't even in the same room. Told Daddy I was going to fall down. Just wait until I got this hick alone. I'd get him out with that soccer ball. Then we'd see who fell down.

Gary pulled a T-shirt over his head, and carrying his tennis shoes and socks, headed for the door. "We'll be waitin' in the truck. Don't go pokin' around too long, let's get this show on the road."

Irritated, I yanked my clothes off and slung them at my suitcases. After I dressed in a fresh outfit, I started for the door, then stopped.

Just because Gary was an ill-mannered slob was no excuse for me to act the same. I went back and neatly folded the garments I'd thrown across the room. The second suitcase only contained the "overflow" from the one Mother couldn't close. I took the few outfits that were there and laid them neatly on the bed. Once we returned home, I could hang them in the closet. For now, the suitcase would serve as a dirty clothes hamper.

When I knelt down to put my clothes in the suitcase, I saw the two rolls of film from last Christmas and the unexposed roll that I had planned to put in the camera. A shudder of guilt raced through me. Quickly I grabbed the camera from the dresser where I'd put it last night. I snapped two quick pictures—

close-ups—then rewound the roll of exposed film and took it out. I put in the new roll, dropped the exposed one in the little case, and snapped the plastic lid shut. I grabbed one of the two rolls of quarters I'd brought along, in the event that there really was a video-game room in Lawton, then raced down the hall and charged out the front door.

But just as I got to the door . . .

WHAM!

Something hit me. Or I hit something. I'm not sure which. I bounced backward. Staggered to catch my balance.

Gary stood in the doorway. There was a startled look on his face. "Man, you're pretty solid for a wussy, city kid." He blinked a couple of times and shook his head as if recovering from the impact of our sudden collision. "Oh," he said, as though remembering why he'd come. "You comin' or not? We're all out in the truck, waitin'."

As I followed him down the stairs I could hear him muttering: "Musta been puttin' on his makeup or somethin'. Don't even take Mama that long to get ready to go. Man, what a klutz."

If my eyes had been lasers, they would have bored a hole through the back of his thick skull.

Just wait until I get you alone, I thought. Just wait until I get you out with the soccer ball. When we get back home, I'd show this moron a thing or two.

I didn't have to wait until we got home.

CHAPTER 8

The town of Lawton actually *did* have a mall. In the mall, there actually *was* a game room. It was small and most of the games were old—almost what I'd consider antiques—but they worked. After we purchased my blue jeans, some T-shirts, and two pair of tennis shoes that fit, Patricia wanted to do a bit of shopping on her own. I challenged Gary to Air Combat.

Just as I suspected, he was a total boob when it came to video games. He didn't have the slightest idea how to operate the flight simulator game or the missile launchers. He was late every time he punched the machine guns. On my turn, I went through at least fifteen enemy planes and tanks and stayed in the flight simulator for a good five to ten minutes. Gary did well to last thirty seconds. He was horrible. In fact, he was such an idiot, he didn't even realize how terrible he was.

"Man, you're good at this stuff." He sounded gleeful and excited. "Let's do 'er again."

The second time on Air Combat, he kept fighting the thing. He leaned the wrong way or pushed against it instead of just going with the flow. It didn't seem to deter his enthusiasm, so we played Cyber Sled next. Gary was even worse at the old, simple games like Ms. Pac Man.

After an hour or so I was totally bored with the lack of competition and ready to leave. Gary wanted to play something else, but I was tired of wasting my quarters on him, so I insisted that we locate his mother.

Lawton Central Mall was virtually deserted, and it took us no time to locate Patricia. She was ready to leave, so we drove to Daddy's photo studio. He insisted on showing me around. It was a small establishment, so it didn't take long. I tried to act interested when Daddy showed me the color developing vats and all the various printers and equipment. When he finished, we went to eat at Red Lobster. I had to sit next to Gary. It was most embarrassing. Out in public, Patricia and Daddy were well-mannered. Gary, on the other hand, ate with his elbows on the table. When he finished his salad, there was more lettuce circling where his plate had been than there was in his stomach. Finally, he used his cheese biscuit to scoop up the butter from his empty shrimp scampi dish. Eating next to him was disgusting.

Daddy hopped out of the truck when we got back to his shop, and Patricia scooted over to drive. I was glad because Gary was practically sitting on my lap in the narrow cab. When he moved, I could finally breathe.

"Why don't you take the boys on home, Pat." Daddy leaned in through the open window and gave her a peck on the cheek. "Don't take the Refuge road. I want to save that for Saturday so I can be with Sam when he sees it for the first time. Pick me up around five-thirty or six?"

She nodded and kissed him on the cheek.

Daddy stepped back and waved as we backed out. We were almost to the street when he came trotting after us. Patricia stopped.

"Almost forgot." He leaned into the truck. "You did bring some film for us to develop, didn't you, Sam?"

I jerked. Uncomfortable, I wiggled down in the seat. "Yes. But it's not with me."

"That's no problem." Daddy smiled. "I've got a shop at the house. When you get home, be sure and put your film out on the kitchen table. That way we won't forget to develop some of it tonight. How many rolls did you bring?"

I ducked my head and cleared my throat.

"Three."

There was a long pause.

"Just three?"

"Yes, sir." I couldn't look at him. "Three is . . . ah . . . well, it's all I haven't had developed yet."

I tried to smile when I looked at my daddy. The corners of his mouth drooped, but he managed to smile back at me. "Three's fine. I'm sure, when we take you out in the Refuge, you'll find a ton of stuff to shoot. We'll develop the three rolls tonight." He turned and headed toward his office. "See you guys this evening."

The guilt that enveloped me was like a fog. Daddy was so proud of the camera he'd sent me, I simply couldn't tell him that three rolls were *all* I had taken the whole time I had the camera. I'd lied to him about that stupid prize thing Mother told him about over the phone, too. I just couldn't stop lying.

Guess that's the trouble with a lie—once it starts, it just seems to grow like a fuzzball in an old vacuum cleaner. From that moment on, I decided I would never lie to my daddy again. When he got home this evening, I would either tell him the truth about the film and the contest—*or*—or keep my mouth shut!

Maybe keeping my mouth shut would be best, I argued with myself. Be still. Be silent. Don't say a word.

We drove for a few minutes. At a stoplight on the four-lane, Gary leaned forward and looked up through the windshield. "We ain't gonna have time to make the fishin' hole and back 'fore dark," he announced. "Reckon we could play some of that there soccer stuff. That all right with you, Sammy?"

Patricia cleared her throat and glanced at him.

"What?" I asked.

"You wanna play soccer when we get home?"

"Sure." I turned away so he couldn't see the sly, evil smile on my face.

At the house we put our things away and I changed into my soccer shoes and my Umbros. On the way outside, I put my three rolls of film on the kitchen table. Gary tucked the soccer ball under his arm and led the way out the back door.

This was the first time I'd ever been out the back. The view was breathtaking. I stopped in my tracks.

The backyard was only about twenty feet wide. It was covered with bright green Bermuda grass. About a quarter of a mile beyond, a jagged mountain rose into the blue Oklahoma sky. It wasn't very tall but the peak was sharp with sheer-faced cliffs. Below the summit, round granite boulders were strewn between small oak trees. Some of the rocks, smooth and round as baseballs, were as big as Mrs. Pipton's carriage house.

And between the narrow backyard and the mountain, there was ABSOLUTELY NOTHING AT ALL. Just empty space where the land seemed to fall away.

Daddy's house was built on the edge of a canyon. I walked toward the edge.

Below me in the distance I could see a wide flat area. More of the enormous boulders were strewn around. There were trees and grass and—

"Stop!"

Gary yelled.

I moved closer to the edge. It was a long way down to the floor of the canyon. I took another step.

"STOP!"

CHAPTER 9

*T*he first time Gary yelled for me to stop, I slowed down. The second time he didn't yell, he screamed! I froze.

Suddenly he was beside me. I felt him grab my arm.

"Man, that's a fifty-foot drop," he said, pulling me away from the edge. "Straight down! You don't never want to get that close."

"I just wanted to see."

"Fine." He made me back up another step. "You can look down from here, but don't you never get no closer. You pitch off the edge, there wouldn't be enough of you left to scrape up with a shovel. Dad would have my hide if you went and fell off."

He continued to cling to my arm as I scanned the valley below. A small, clear stream wove its way through the center. In spots, it sparkled white with small rapids. In other places, the water was smooth where the stream widened into shimmering pools. It was so clear, I could see rocks and pebbles at the bottom, even from way up here.

"It's spectacular," I breathed.

"Yeah, it's purty." Gary tugged at my arm. "Let's go play soccer."

I pulled back. "Can we go down there and look around? Can we go explore? How do you get down?"

"There's a path about fifty feet the other side of the house." He answered. "But it takes a long time to get down. It's a dangerous climb, too. We ain't got time today. I'll take ya down tomorrow. Now, come on."

He pulled on my arm again. Reluctantly, I followed him. To the right of the back porch the yard widened into an open expanse of short but thick grass. A small path led across it to a rustic barn. Beside the barn was a small, shabby-looking little shed.

"Reckon this is about the biggest flat place we got on the whole property," Gary said, gesturing around at the area in front of the barn. "Used to be the old cow lot, 'fore we moved here. Ain't too many big rocks and stuff for you to trip over. Figure it's big enough for a soccer field?"

Ain't too many big rocks and stuff for you to trip over. The words throbbed in my ears. I turned my attention from the canyon to glare at Gary. Inside my head I could hear my teeth grinding together. We'll see who spends more time falling down, I mused.

"It should be big enough." I smiled.

49

"Okay." Gary smiled back. "So how do you play this stuff?"

"Well, each team has a goal at either end of the field," I began. "There's eleven players on a team—"

"Oh, just like football," he interrupted. "I know how to play football."

"Not quite."

He frowned. "Two goals. Eleven players. Sounds like football. All ya gotta do is get the ball across the goal, right?"

"No." I felt my eyes roll inside my head. "You have to *kick* the ball through the goal. It has to go between the cross bars and—"

"Oh. Like kickin' a field goal?" He gave me that goofy smile again. "In other words, you grab the ball and run down the field, only instead of runnin' it over the goal line, you drop it and kick a field goal."

"You don't *run* the ball. You have to dribble it."

Gary took the ball from under his arm and started bouncing it.

"Yeah." He grinned. "Like basketball. Sure, I can do that."

I stood and watched in utter amazement as he dribbled past me. Weaving back and forth, he bounced the ball across the yard. About twenty feet in front of the barn, he stopped and caught it. Then he punted the thing through the upper level loft and into the barn. Elated, he slapped his hands together so loudly that it sounded like a gunshot. Then he spun to face me.

"Hey! How about that? Made a touchdown, first shot off the bat. Pretty good, huh?"

My mouth had gaped so wide, I had to put my hand under my chin and close it. If I hadn't, I would have tripped over my bottom lip when I walked toward him.

Gary was still bouncing around like a frisky puppy when I stopped in front of him.

"You believe I made a touchdown that easy? I'm gonna be a natural at this soccer stuff, ain't I? Done good, huh?"

"Done good," I answered, mocking him. "Only trouble is, you can't use your hands."

"Huh?"

"You can't touch the ball with your hands."

"Then how do you dribble?"

"Just go get the ball out of the barn." I sighed. "I'll show you."

"Okay," he said, "but remember, don't get too near the cliff."

Trying to teach Gary how to play soccer was like trying to teach an alley cat how to sit, roll over, and come when you call. It was next to impossible.

I spent an hour showing him how to dribble and pass the ball. It took nearly half that time just to get him to pass the ball with the inside of his foot instead of toe-punching the thing. Every ten minutes, he kept reminding me not to get too near the cliff.

He was just as dopey when it came to dribbling. He

had no control whatsoever. He'd simply kick the ball out in front of him, then race to catch it so he could kick it again. Finally, realizing there was no hope, I suggested we go in and get something to drink.

"Nah. This is fun," the idiot said. "Let's play a real game."

"It's not fun. It's boring," I insisted. "And you're not ready for a game. Let's go in."

"Ah, come on. You're not chicken, are ya?"

The stupid grin on his face seemed to stretch from ear to ear. I shrugged. It'd serve him right.

There were two double doors on the front of the barn. We opened one of them. The opening was taller than a regular soccer goal but not quite as wide. I gave Gary the ball first. He started in the middle of the field, I stole it and made a goal. Same thing the second time, then the third, then . . .

Gary spent most of his time inside the barn, retrieving the soccer ball. It was like playing one-on-one against a second grader. Within ten minutes it was eight to nothing. It didn't take long before I was so bored, I quit stealing the ball and just kicked it away from him so he'd have to go chase it. I felt like I was going to be stuck with this idiot for the rest of my life. Two weeks of this was going to be more than an eternity.

Then it dawned on me. If I kicked the ball over the edge of the cliff . . .

What had Gary said? "Fifty-foot straight drop . . . Takes us too long to get down . . . I'll take you down tomorrow." Smiling, I waited for him to dribble toward me once more.

Sure enough, here he came. As usual, the ball was way too far in front of him. I held my spot until he kicked it again, then I darted for it and booted the thing. The soccer ball sailed toward the cliff and the canyon below. It bounced. It rolled. Then right on the edge, the darned thing stopped.

I shot a blast of air up my forehead. Just my luck.

"I got 'er," Gary called, racing for the ball. Only when he reached the ball, instead of kicking it, he bent down to pick it up. He stumbled. As he straightened to turn toward me, I noticed the strange expression on his face. Eyes wide and mouth open as if to scream, he staggered backward.

Suddenly he dropped the ball. Both arms began to spin round and round like the blades of a windmill as he tried to catch his balance. He was right at the edge of the cliff. I could see the panic on his face as he teetered.

He reached out toward me.

Then ... then he was gone.

I heard a scream. A long, terrified scream that grew faint and distant as Gary plummeted into the gaping abyss, just beyond my view.

The breath caught in my throat. I couldn't breathe. My legs wouldn't move. My heart pounded in my ears. Then a tiny voice seemed to scream from inside my head:

Samuel! What have you done?

And before I could even make my feet move, before I could take that first trembling step toward the cliff, that same inner voice answered:

You've killed Gary!

Frantic, I raced toward the edge where he had vanished. After only a few strides, my knees locked. I froze, unable to move. In my mind's eye I could see the sight below. It was too graphic—too horrible to think about. I tried to chase the image from my head but it wouldn't leave.

I forced my legs to move. I ran again, then stopped. As I neared the edge, I took one step at a time. Then, inch by inch, I scooted closer. I didn't want to see what I had done to Gary.

But I had to.

As I stretched my neck and peered over, I realized the sight below would stay with me . . . *forever.*

CHAPTER 10

*G*ary!

The top of his head was less than two feet below the edge of the cliff. He looked up, and that stupid, goofy grin stretched clear across his ugly face.

"Gotcha!"

Then he started to laugh.

Confused and frantic, my eyes darted about like a wild bird caught in a snare. Gary stood on a narrow rock ledge about six feet below the edge of the cliff. The outcrop of rock was only some four feet wide, but it ran the entire length of the ridge. Like a hidden path, it came from near the little shed by the barn on my right, clear across to disappear into rocks on the far side of the back porch.

"Wish I had a picture." He pointed at me. "Man, the look on your face—you ought to see it. I can't believe—" He was laughing so hard, he couldn't even finish a sentence.

"What a sucker! You went for the fallin' off the cliff bit, hook, line, and sinker. What a face . . . what a . . ."

I glared down at him, shaking. At first I had trembled from fear for what I thought I had done. Now my shaking was from sheer fury.

Gary was lucky that the soccer ball was the only thing I could find. If there had been a boulder or a club, I would have used that. As it was . . .

I pelted him with the soccer ball. I threw it as hard as I could. The thing hit the top of his head. It was a glancing blow that sent the ball sailing far out into empty space. It fell and fell and fell, taking forever to finally hit a big flat rock at the floor of the valley. It bounced twice and landed in the branches of a little oak tree. Gary laughed.

A puff of red burst before my eyes. If I could just get hold of him—just get my hands on him for one minute—if I could only find something big enough and hard enough to hit him with . . .

I was going to kill Gary.

"Well, where are they?" I heard Daddy's voice, then the sound of the front screen bounce shut.

"Gary's outside," Patricia answered. "I told him to get the ball and *not* to come in the house until we came back from town."

"Sam?"

"He's upstairs."

I sat on the edge of the bed and waited. I could

hear footsteps coming. A board on the wooden steps squeaked. When Daddy appeared at the doorway to the bedroom, I stood and picked up my bags from the floor.

"I'm going home," I announced. "Will you please drive me to the airport?"

Daddy took a deep breath, followed by a long sigh. He sat on the edge of the bed and patted the mattress for me to sit beside him.

"Patricia told me what happened," he said. "I'd like to hear your version."

I was a bit reluctant to put my suitcases down, but I did. I sat beside Daddy and told him about the horrible thing Gary had done. When I finished, he asked me to wait while he went to hear what Gary had to say. "It's only fair to hear his version, too."

I sat on the edge of the bed until I heard Daddy call Gary in from outside. Then I crept to the open doorway. I couldn't see the bottom of the stairs from there, but I could hear the voices as they drifted up the staircase.

"I was just funnin' with him," Gary whined. "When Robert and me get together or when Garth comes over, we're all the time doin' stuff like that. You know, playin' tricks on each other. There's no harm in it. How's I to know he'd get so bent outta shape?"

"You and Robert and Garth play together a lot. You go to school together. You know each other."

"Sam doesn't know you that well." Patricia joined the conversation. "He's a guest in our home and he's only been here one night. That falling off the cliff bit was totally uncalled for."

"It wasn't all that bad," I heard Gary protest. "That Sammy just got no sense of humor."

"No sense of humor," Patricia yelped. "You think falling off a fifty-foot cliff is supposed to be funny? You think breaking your fool neck or scaring somebody as bad as you scared Sam"—her voice grew louder and louder—"you think that's supposed to make him double over laughing?"

"No, ma'am," Gary's voice was soft. I leaned farther out the doorway so I could hear. "I reckon it wasn't too smart a thing to do."

"Smart?" Patricia huffed. "It was downright mean. Cruel. Your father and I both want you boys to hit it off. We asked you to be on your best behavior—to be nice to him. Do you remember?"

"Yes, ma'am. but Sammy ain't been the easiest person to get along with. He ain't been all that nice to me."

"Just what does that mean?" Daddy asked.

"And what is it with all this *ain't* stuff?" Patricia asked before Gary could answer. "You don't normally use that word. You trying to impress Sam? Or are you just trying to sound like a total idiot?"

"What do you mean, he ain't been all that nice?" Daddy repeated.

I tiptoed from the room. At the top of the staircase I held the banister and leaned around the corner. I still couldn't see them, but I could hear better.

"He took me to that game room at the mall and beat the tar out of me," Gary said. "He knew I ain't never—" He stopped and I could hear him clear his throat. "He knew I hadn't ever played those games before. But he didn't tell me how to do anything or how to work the controls. He just beat me. And I tried to act nice—like I was having a good time, but it sure wasn't much fun. And when we got home, I took him out to play with the soccer ball. I told him I'd never played soccer. It's a stupid game. Nobody around here ever plays soccer. But I tried to learn and act like it was fun. Sammy showed me a little bit about it, but like the game room, mostly, he just beat the tar out of me. And . . . and . . . ."

"And?" Daddy urged.

"And he acts like he's smarter and better than all of us. He goes around trying to make me feel like I'm dumb. And maybe I am, but he don't have to keep being so snooty or treating me like I was dirt. I mean . . . well, shoot, if it come a good rainstorm, his nose is stuck up so high in the air, he'd probably drown."

There was a long silence. I scooted away from the staircase, retreating to the doorway of our room.

"Sam," Daddy called.

"Yes, sir."

"Come on down here. I need to talk with both of you."

I picked up my suitcases and, straining against the weight, managed to tote them down the stairs. Daddy's shoulders sagged when he saw me carrying the bags.

"Can I go home now?"

He took one and we all went into the living room. Daddy sat in the recliner. He motioned to the couch. I sat on one end, Gary sat on the other, and Patricia put herself between us.

"First off," Daddy began, "the only way I could afford to bring you here from Connecticut was to buy one of those Super Saver specials from the airlines. Now, I've done business with the airlines before. To get the ticket, you have to have an over-Saturday-night stay. What that means is you're going to have to stay here until next Sunday or we're going to have to buy you a new ticket.'

"Couldn't I fly standby?"

Daddy shook his head. "From my experience, with a Super Saver, neither an act of Congress nor an act of God would be enough to get the airline to change their policy. So you're stuck here, at least until Sunday." He cleared his throat and looked first at me then at Gary. "I think you boys just got off to a bad start. The way things are going, you'll either have to work out your differences, or you're going to kill each other by the end of the week. My vote is for working things out. How about you two?"

CHAPTER 11

When adults vote, kids don't stand a chance. It's just not fair.

Daddy voted to work things out. So did Patricia. Gary and I just sat there. After a while we both leaned forward so we could see around Patricia and glare at each other. Then Daddy *told us* we were going to resolve our differences.

It was almost dark when he finished. Patricia left to prepare supper. Gary and I listened, and although somewhat reluctant, we agreed with most of what Daddy told us. We didn't have all that much choice. Like I said, he was an "adult."

Gary agreed not to play any more tricks on me, and I confessed that I had overreacted. I must admit, I did lose my head a bit. Chasing Gary around the house with the shovel was, perhaps, a little much. I also apologized for not helping him with the video games, and I promised that the next time we played soccer, I would show him how to dribble and pass the ball instead of simply beating him to a pulp. Gary said he had planned to take me fishing tomorrow, and he promised Daddy he would help me instead of not showing or telling me what to do.

After supper Daddy told me to pick up my three rolls of film and follow him out to the little shed beside the barn. Daddy said it had been a chicken coop, but he'd totally remodeled it and turned it into a darkroom. He'd put in electricity and a gas stove to keep the developing chemicals at the proper temperature.

I noticed a horrid smell as soon as the three of us entered the small building. It was a pungent odor that made my nose crinkle.

"What is that?" I coughed.

Daddy fanned his face and opened the door. He pushed Gary and me back. Holding his breath, he trotted through the small room and opened the back door.

"Butane," he answered from the other end of the small room. "I've got a gas leak in the stove that I've been meaning to fix. It's usually not this bad, but I just filled the butane tank." He fanned his face again. "Shoooie."

We waited outside for the gas smell to clear out of the room. Then we went into the darkroom and developed two rolls of my film. They were the ones I took the first Christmas I had the camera. It didn't take all that much time, but since we had spent so long "discussing" our problems with Daddy, it was quite late.

Daddy hung the film to dry. "We'll get your third roll tomorrow," he said. "I'm sleepy. Let's go in."

Beside the doorway there was a round table. On top of the table was a glass fishbowl. The thing was enormous and filled clear to the brim with rolls of film. Before we left for the house, Daddy had me put my last roll on top of the pile.

"Didn't realize I was so far behind on my developing," Daddy said. "Be sure and put your film on the very top. That way it won't get mixed in with all the other rolls."

As I put my film in the bowl, I noticed a BB gun leaning against the doorjamb behind the table. It looked just like the one Justin Porter had back home.

"Gary, is that your gun?" I asked.

Gary had been quiet most of the time we were in the developing room with Daddy. (I was thankful for that.) He glanced at where I was pointing and shook his head.

"Nope. It's Dad's." He gave a little laugh. "We call it the Rescue Rifle."

I looked up at Daddy. He had a rather sheepish look on his face. I hesitated at the door. Finally Daddy shrugged.

"Well," he said, and made a gulping sound when he swallowed. "You know how I feel about guns. I'd lots rather take a picture of some animal than shoot it. But ... well, there's a skunk that lives somewhere around the barn and . . . ah, one night, when I started to leave the darkroom and go inside . . . well, the darned thing got me."

"Got ya good," Gary agreed. "Mom wouldn't let him in the house for two days. You talk about stink!"

Daddy cleared his throat. "Well, anyway . . . about two weeks later, he was back again. Every time I'd try to get out of the darkroom, he'd come bouncing toward me and spin around, like he was gonna spray me. Ended up spending most of the night out here. It was four o'clock in the morning before Pat woke up and noticed I was missing. She and Gary had to come rescue me."

"That's why we call 'er the Rescue Rifle," Gary said. "Dad works kinda late some nights. Mom and I are usually in bed, and if the skunk comes around, all Dad's gotta do is pop him in the butt with a BB. He can rescue himself instead of waiting for us to wake up and come after him."

Daddy turned off the light and closed the door. On the way to the house, he put one arm around my shoulder and the other around Gary.

"I think the world of you two boys," he said proudly. "I figure, once you get to know one another, you're gonna really be good friends."

Gary and I didn't respond.

"Things will be better tomorrow. You'll see."

The way Daddy said it, I wasn't sure whether he meant it as an optimistic promise—or a *threat*. Whatever, Gary and I both agreed that we'd try to get along.

It had been a long, long day. I dressed for bed and crawled under the sheets. For the first time since I left home, I slept well. In fact, I snoozed like a baby, until . . .

KER-WHAM! KABOOOM!

CHAPTER 12

One moment I was sound asleep. The next I was on my feet in the doorway to the bedroom.

How I got there, I had no idea. What I was thinking—where I was going—I had no inkling.

I blinked and looked around. The morning dawn that filtered in through the windows was so dim I could hardly see.

It was a dream, I thought. I shook my head. No, I heard something. Shivering, I took a deep breath and listened. Maybe Patricia and Daddy were awake. Perhaps they were in the kitchen and had dropped something or . . .

Ker-whomp! KABOOOM!

The explosion rattled the windows. The rumbling that followed was so deep and powerful, it shook my chest.

An explosion. A bomb. The muscles tightened across my shoulders. My hands tightened to fists. Then I knew what it was. The butane smell from last night . . . Daddy's dark room had exploded.

Ker-whomp! KABOOOM!

Again the blast rattled the windows. Startled and near panic, I looked around the room.

Gary was still sleeping. He lay there with his mouth open, snoozing as if he hadn't even heard the repeated explosions. I raced to the side of his bed. Shook him. Gary moaned and rolled away from me. I reached across his bed and shook him again.

"Gary! Gary, wake up."

He moaned and forced his eyes open.

"Huh? What?"

"Explosion . . . the darkroom . . . blew up . . ."

Ker-whomp! KABOOM!

I jumped again. "Did you hear it? There it was again. It—It—"

Gary sat up. He yawned so wide, you could have driven a small Audi into the gaping cavern of his mouth. "What 'er you shakin' me for? What are you blabbin' about?"

"Explosions—bombs or something—listen."

He shook his head, blinked a couple of times and waited.

Ker-whomp! KABOOM!

I knew he *had* to hear it that time. He was awake enough that there was no way he could have missed the sound. Excited, I pointed to the window that still vibrated from the explosion. I expected Gary to be just as startled and excited as I was. Instead, he sneered at me. Disgusted, he shook his head and flopped back on his pillow.

"It's Fort Sill," he groaned. "I can't believe you woke me up."

"It's Fort what? What was it?"

"Fort Sill." He tried to wrap his pillow around his face and ears. "They're practicin'."

I grabbed the pillow and jerked it from his head. He reached for it, but I held it out of his grasp. "There are explosions! Something is blowing up. What is it?"

Exasperated, Gary sat up in bed and rubbed his eyes.

"It's the army's artillery school." He yawned. "Fort Sill is a military base. That's where they practice shootin' off their cannons—you know, howitzer? Artillery? Big guns? You know what I'm talking about? They're target-practicin' out in the West Range. That's all they're doin'. They do it all the time. Ain't no big deal. Now give me my pillow."

Ker-whomp! KERBOOOM!

The windows shook. I felt the vibration in my chest. "You mean, that goes on all the time?"

"Well, mostly not on weekends. You'll get used to it. Folks what lived 'round here long as we have don't even notice it." Again he reached for his pillow.

"It sounds like it's right outside the window. You don't *notice* that?"

Gary shook his head. "Don't even hear it, most of the time. And it's not right outside the window. Range is about two miles the other side of Mount Scott—

good six miles from here." He made one last grab for his pillow. Then, after kicking the sheets off, he sat up. "Now you done got me awake. We might as well go fishin'."

After we dressed, I followed Gary downstairs. Much to my disbelief, Daddy and Patricia were still asleep. Gary prepared a bowl of cereal and milk for both of us. While we ate, I could still hear the explosions. There would be long periods of silence, followed by three to five Ker-whomp! KERBOOOMs! It didn't seem as loud or frightening as before. I guess that was partially because we were in a different area of the house and partially because I now knew what the sound really was. After we ate, Gary led the way to the back porch. Stacked in the corner next to the washer and dryer were fishing rods and reels. He pulled out five, leaned each of them against the side of the screened porch and inspected the lines. Then he selected two and put the others back in the corner. Next, he practically stood on his head to lean over the washing machine. He dug around and finally retrieved an orange plastic box with a handle on it.

"Mepp's spinners is probably the best thing there is for sand bass." He dug around in the box and handed me six small silver things with feathers on the ends. "Reckon three each oughta last us. Watch the hooks."

Naturally he said "watch the hooks" after I had already closed my fingers around them. My hand sprung open as the sharp barbs bit into my palm and the tips of my fingers.

69

"Better take a package of hooks, too," he said, folding something and stuffing it into his pocket. "If the sand bass ain't runnin', it's a long walk to come back empty-handed. We might catch some bait and get us a couple of perch."

He had me drop the six "spinners" into a paper bag that he then wadded up and stuffed into his pocket. He handed me a fishing rod, and we were off.

Once outside the back door, Gary turned to the left. I followed him to the edge of the cliff, where he jumped down to the ledge. I trailed behind him and remembered yesterday and how scared I was when I saw him fall and how angry I became when I realized he'd tricked me. Well, seeing the ledge that ran along the face of the cliff made me mad all over again.

We followed the ledge for some thirty feet to a stand of tall trees. They were about the only *tall* trees I'd seen since I arrived. There the ledge disappeared into a pile of loose rock. Leading the way down the steep slope, Gary leaped from one large stone to the next. I wasn't quite as agile on the rocks, nor was I accustomed to my new tennis shoes. So instead of leaping, I stepped carefully from one boulder to the next. We moved cautiously and slowly toward the bottom of the canyon. At times the rocks and huge stones were so far apart and the drop between them was so steep, I had to sit on my bottom and stretch out my legs to get from one level to the next. Gary bounded on ahead and patiently waited for me from time to time.

Finally, after twenty minutes or so, we reached the floor of the valley. A flat area stretched out before us. On the right, the cliff where the house was loomed above. Gary had at least told me the truth about that. Aside from the ledge that ran just below the summit, the cliff was a straight drop. It was easily fifty feet high. I was amazed that we had accomplished the descent so quickly.

I followed Gary toward the little stream. The valley floor was flat but strewn with rocks. Some of the stones were smooth and round, others jagged and rough. Once, I slipped and fell. Quickly I scrambled to my feet, hoping Gary hadn't noticed.

He stopped on top of a large boulder about twenty feet ahead of me. He turned and I couldn't help but notice that sloppy, goofy smile on his face.

"Almost forgot," he said. "Be sure and watch out for rattlesnakes."

CHAPTER 13

*T*he journey to the fishing spot would have been difficult enough, what with the rocks and boulders and driftwood logs and dead tree limbs—everything imaginable to climb and trip over as we moved along the little stream. What made it worse were my new tennis shoes weren't broken in. We were still within view of the path down the cliff, and I could already feel the blisters rubbing on my heels. Then, on top of all that . . .

Every single step I took, I expected to find a rattlesnake beneath my foot.

At first, because of the goofy smile on Gary's face, I had my suspicions that he might have made up the caution about rattlesnakes. But the farther we moved down the canyon and the more rugged the area became, I realized that this was indeed the perfect terrain to find the poisonous beasts. My fear slowed my progress even more than the unfamiliar ground beneath my feet.

We must have traveled for over an hour before the narrow stream we were following began to widen. There were places where the water was shallow. It bubbled white and shimmered in the morning sunlight as it danced over the rocks. Farther down, the stream widened and smoothed a bit, although from the swirls and eddies on the surface, I could tell the current was still quite strong.

We rounded a sharp bend in the riverbed, and in the distance there was suddenly no more stream. Instead, a blue, glistening lake spread out before us. Its surface was smooth, the water clear and bright.

" 'Bout another hundred yards or so," Gary called over his shoulder. "That's where we oughta find 'em if they're runnin'."

I noticed Gary was no longer waiting for me. He scurried ahead, hopping from one rock to the next until he worked his way down the flat above the river to stand next to the bank. A sandbar, composed mostly of small, gravel-like rock, stretched before him. He dug in his pocket and pulled out the paper sack. Frantic fingers tied one of the little spinners onto the end of his fishing line.

"Hurry up," he called over his shoulder. "I'll show ya how to tie your spinner on. Then yer on yer own."

When I reached him, Gary practically yanked the rod and reel from my hand. Despite his instructions as he worked, Gary tied the spinner on so quickly, I had no idea how he'd done it. He shoved the rod and reel back into my hand, then trotted to the edge of the sandbar.

The tip of the gravel jetty where he stood was in a bend of the river. A sheer rock cliff was on the opposite side of the stream. Between the jetty and the cliff the water was forced into a narrow channel that made the current churn and swirl.

"Ever been fishin' 'fore?"

Confidently, I nodded.

Gary nodded back. "Well, get after it."

He began throwing his little spinner, time and again, across the swift current. I stood watching, then tried it myself.

I brought the rod back over my shoulder, as Gary did. I brought my arm forward quickly, to send the little sliver spinner sailing into the blue sky.

Nothing happened.

The little silver thing still dangled from the tip of my rod. I tried it again.

Still nothing.

Gary looked back at me. His mouth twisted up on one side. "Thought you said you'd been fishin' before?"

I nodded—not quite so confident this time.

"Randall took me deep-sea fishing off Nantucket one time. We went again when we were down in Florida. But it wasn't like this."

He frowned. "How come?"

I tried to throw the plug again. Still nothing happened. "Well," I began, "for one thing, the boat crew baited the hooks for us. Then they threw the line out and we waited for something to happen."

"You catch anything?"

"An amberjack."

Gary cocked an eyebrow. "And I suppose they even took it off the hook for you."

"As a matter of fact, they did."

"Figures." Gary threw his rod and reel down in the gravel at his feet. "Pay attention. I'm only gonna do this once or twice." He moved behind me and reached around. With his hand wrapped about the back of mine, he raised the rod. "See that little black button. Push 'er with your thumb and hold 'er down." He brought the tip of the rod above and behind us. "When you whip the rod forward, you let your thumb up—that frees the line."

The little silver spinner sailed way out into the stream and landed with a tiny plop.

"Now, all you gots to do is reel it in."

I seized one of the small black knobs on the handle and began retrieving my spinner. When it was back to the tip of the rod, Gary said, "Now, you try it on your own."

I raised my arm, pushed the black button down, and as I brought it forward, the spinner sailed out and . . . went *splat* right at my feet!

"Didn't let your thumb up quick enough," Gary observed. "Try 'er once more."

I did as he instructed, this time making sure to release my thumb earlier. The plug sailed into the blue sky . . . straight above our heads. Then it plummeted down, coming right for us. I jumped out of the way, just in the nick of time.

"What happened that time?"

Gary tried to wipe the goofy smile from his face. "Let go too early. Got to get somewheres in between." He turned to retrieve his rod. "You're gettin' the hang of it, though. 'Bout fifty more casts, you ought to be able to hit that little spinner where you're aimin'."

I was proud of myself. As Gary had put it, I got the hang of it, and much more rapidly than he had expected. After just a few casts I fell into a rhythm of casting my plug and reeling it back in. Once my casts were mastered, there was time to more or less sit back and enjoy myself. A small mountain rose in the distance. The top was round and smooth. Every now and then I could see the reflection from a car up there. When I inquired about it, Gary told me that it was Mount Scott. He said there was a road where people could drive to the top and enjoy the scenery. The water out in the lake was so smooth and flat, I could see the reflection of the mountain in spots. The scenery was breathtaking.

Maybe this fishing stuff wasn't so bad, after all.

In fact, I was really starting to enjoy myself. I was having fun. Everything was progressing exceptionally well, until . . .

I caught a fish.

Chapter 14

*W*hat happened?"

Even from the doorway of our bedroom, I could hear the tension, irritation, and anxiety in Daddy's voice.

"Everything!" Patricia answered.

"Tell me about the house and the car, first," Daddy urged.

"Well, I got home from my doctor's appointment about four-thirty. Gary was already here. He was acting real excited and nervous. He said he was coming up the path from the bottom of the cliff and heard a door slam. Then he heard car doors shutting. As he topped the ridge he claims he saw a big black car driving off. He just *knows* somebody was in the house."

"Anything missing?"

"Not that we can find," Patricia answered. "Gary and I looked the place over pretty well. There's no sign of anybody prying a window open or jimmying the doors. But the front door was unlocked." She sighed. "I know I locked the house before I left. I'm sure of it."

There was a long silence. I slipped from the open doorway to listen at the top of the stairs.

"Nothing missing," Daddy reflected. "No sign of a break-in. Just the front door unlocked."

"That's right. But when I was coming home, 'bout three miles up the road, I did see a black sedan. There were some men in it, but I didn't pay any attention. Not until Gary hit me with the somebody-was-in-the-house stuff and told me about the black car. Well, it was enough to make me just a little edgy. That—along with the boys—well, maybe I shouldn't have called you. I know you planned to work late tonight and—"

"No, hon," he interrupted. "You did the right thing. Now what about the boys?"

Again there was a long silence. I crouched down on one knee, hoping to see them at the bottom of the stairs.

Patricia cleared her throat.

"Well, the whole thing might just have been Gary's way of covering his tracks for running off and leaving Sam. I mean, if I hadn't seen the car, that's exactly what I would have figured he was up to. I just don't know . . ."

"What happened?"

"Well, like I said, Gary was here when I got home from the doctor's. With all the excitement from his black car story, I didn't even notice Sam was missing until right before I called you.

"Seems like they fished for a couple of hours. They were doing fine until they started catching fish, then Gary got upset with Sam because he had to take the fish off Sam's hook. I'm not sure about the details, but he finally got mad and ran off and left Sam."

I heard a squeak when the front door opened.

"*Gary!*" Daddy's voice boomed so loud it made me jump. "Get in here!"

I smiled to myself, hearing the anger in his voice.

"*Sam!*" Daddy roared. I jumped again, but this time the smile on my face dropped clear down to my knees. "Get down here!"

My bags were packed, again. They were at the foot of the bed. This time, when I went down the stairs, I decided it best to leave them behind.

Daddy motioned Gary and me to the couch. But he didn't sit in his recliner like he did the last time we had a "little discussion." Instead he stood right in front of us, put his fists on his hips, and glared down.

"What happened?" he demanded.

Gary admitted that I did pretty well, until . . . I caught a fish. He said he didn't mind taking the first two or three off the hook for me, but got tired of it after about five or six. I told Daddy how I tried—how I even held one or two down with my foot, but couldn't extract the hook. I even showed him the little hole in my hand where one of the sharp fins had brought blood when I tried to hold the fish. Then

Gary explained how he'd told me how to fold the fin down so I wouldn't get stuck, but how he figured I just thought it was easier to get *him* to take the fish off.

That's when the argument erupted.

"I tried my best," I snapped. "I really did."

"Didn't either," Gary snorted. "I been fishing with iddy-biddy kids that can take fish off better than you did." He cocked his eyebrows at Daddy and Patricia. "Sammy just wanted me to wait on him and do all the work. I couldn't even catch a fish 'cause I was so busy with him. Anybody would get fed up!"

"Sam, do you have anything to add?"

"I don't like being called Sammy," I huffed. "Gary knows that. As far as the fishing . . . I did the best I could."

Daddy motioned Patricia to follow him to the kitchen. Gary and I both remained on our respective end of the couch and didn't so much as look at each other.

When they came back, Patricia stood in front of Gary and Daddy stood in front of me.

"I see no excuse for running off and leaving Sam out there. He could have really gotten lost, instead of just missing the path back up the cliff. I think you owe him an apology."

Gary's eyes flashed.

I had to fight to keep the smile from coming to my face. It was all I could do to keep from laughing.

"Samuel!"

I blinked and looked up at Daddy.

"For some strange reason, I doubt that this was entirely Gary's fault. What do you think?"

Before I could answer, Gary leaped up from the couch. "Me apologize?" he yelped. "No way!"

Patricia's eyes narrowed to tight slits. "What did you say, young man?"

Gary slumped back on the couch. "It wasn't my fault," he mumbled.

This time it was Patricia who motioned Daddy to the kitchen.

In a moment or two they came back. Patricia carried a green bundle tucked under her arm. Stopping in front of the couch, she tossed it to Gary. I glanced from the corner of one eye. The bundle was a padded material, tied in a cylinder with black straps. Gary looked down at it, then up at his mother. Her smile was neither kind nor sweet.

"If you're not even man enough to admit when you're wrong, you can just take that sleeping bag and stay in the barn till you're ready to apologize."

Daddy's chin jutted out as sharp and rugged as the cliff outside the back door when he glared down at me.

"You can 'want to go home' until you turn blue in the face," he growled. "But you're going up to your room. And you'll stay there till I say otherwise. Now, *move!*"

At first I was mad at Daddy. I thought about crawling out the window with my suitcases and walking to

the airport. If I could have found my camera, I might
have tried it. But for the life of me, I couldn't remember what I had done with the thing. Finally I realized
I could never make it that far with all that Mother
had packed in my bags. Then I got mad at Gary. He
should have apologized. He should have said he was
sorry. It was all his fault.

The sound of pans clanking brought me from the
bed to the doorway. I held my breath, listening.

"Can't believe it's nine-thirty and I'm just now starting supper." Patricia's voice came faint and distant
from the kitchen.

"Well, if Gary and Sam hadn't caused so many
problems, we would have been finished eating by
now," Daddy said. "Why not save it till tomorrow.
I'm not hungry anymore."

"Chicken will spoil if I try to refreeze it or put it
in the refrigerator," Patricia answered. "I'll go ahead
and fry it up." Another pan clanked. "Tomorrow we'll
put it in a casserole or something for lunch."

It's funny what the smell of food can do to a person's mind. Especially when that person has been
fishing and hiking all day and has had nothing to eat
but a bowl of cereal. The smell drifted up the staircase
to tug at my nose.

I lay on the bed, staring up at the ceiling. Maybe I
really had been sort of a pain. In all probability, I
could have gotten the fish off the hook myself. Only
I was having so much fun catching them . . . well, it

was quicker to get Gary to take them off. The smell of supper lingered heavy in the air.

Maybe if I told Daddy that I'd apologize to Gary if Gary would tell me he was sorry first. I shook my head at the thought. Gary would never say he was sorry first. And if he thought I was going to apologize first . . . served him right to have to sleep in the barn.

The food sure smelled good.

Maybe Daddy could count to three and we could both apologize at the same time. I smiled. It was worth a try.

I swung my feet over the edge of the bed and sat up.

Suddenly, the sound of breaking glass ripped through the quiet house. There was a crashing sound.

"What are you doin'? What's goin' on? Who . . ." Daddy's shouts were instantly cut short.

I sprang to my feet.

Men's voices followed—loud, mean, gruff voices.

I ran toward the stairs.

Patricia screamed!

CHAPTER 15

At the staircase, I caught only a glimpse of Daddy. A man grabbed him from behind, as another struggled with him. Then all three disappeared from my line of vision.

There was another man.

His steel-gray eyes focused on me. He bounded up the stairs. I was frozen with the screams and shouts and turmoil from below. I didn't have time to run. I never even thought about it. Like a total idiot, I stood until the man reached the top of the stairs and grabbed the front of my shirt. He lifted me up like I was no heavier than Justin Porter's BB gun. With my feet off the ground, I dangled limply before him. His steel-gray eyes seemed to cut into mine. There was no feeling—no anger—nothing in those eyes. In one easy motion the man tossed my limp body from side to side and flipped me under his arm like a sack of dog food he was carrying to the checkout counter.

I couldn't move. I couldn't scream. I was so petrified with fear that I was halfway down the stairs before I began to kick and fight.

A heavy hand whacked me across the side of the head. My neck bounced down, then popped back up like it was on a spring. My eyes seemed to roll in their sockets.

"I'm not gonna hurt you," a rolling, smooth voice said. "Hold still!"

The way he had me tucked under his arm, the only thing I could see as we went down the stairs and through the living room were his black trousers. When I saw the floor change from carpet to tile, I knew we were in the kitchen. I could hear Patricia crying. Daddy coughed. Then he coughed again.

I strained, trying to see them. But just as I lifted my head, I was spinning again. This time I landed on my bottom. I was flung into one of the kitchen chairs with such force that my eyes crossed and my seat throbbed clear up into my temples.

Once more there were the steel-gray eyes. The man leaned in so close to me that the eyes and the bridge of his nose were all I could see.

"You be real still and quiet, boy." His soft voice was almost a whisper. "Don't move and you won't get hurt."

As he backed away, my eyes darted about the kitchen. Daddy was in a chair next to me. A tall, slender man stood behind him with his hands on Daddy's shoulders. He had sneaky eyes that seemed to dart about the room as quickly and nervously as my eyes did.

Daddy was slumped in his chair, holding his stomach. Another man stood, with clenched fists, in front of his chair. He was a big man—his face ugly. Daddy coughed again and gasped for air. The man in front of him had on a cotton T-shirt. A huge arm stuck out of the sleeve, the muscle in it big and lumpy.

"Try hoppin' up again, ol' buddy," he drawled. "Ain't had my workout today. You're better than a punchin' bag. Come on," he taunted. "Hop up again."

Daddy clutched his stomach and didn't look up.

"That's enough, Ratcliff." A voice from behind me made my head whip around.

Patricia was in a chair across the table. A man stood next to her. He was dark complected, with sunken cheeks. His brown eyes were set so deeply in his head, it was a wonder he could even see. The man looked strangely familiar.

"I think everybody's calm and ready to settle down now." His tone was drippy-sweet, like syrup oozing from a maple tree. "Now that the introductions are over, I'm sure everybody's going to be real still and quiet." His words were so slow and deliberate that all of us looked at him. Even Daddy raised his head and turned.

The man pulled a chair over and sat down next to Patricia. He reached into the pocket of his silk coat and pulled something out. I only got a glimpse of the white, pearl handle as he moved toward Patricia. There was a soft, yet distinct click.

A silver blade sprang from the pearl handle. It glistened and sparkled in the light. As casual and relaxed as someone holding an ink pen, he twisted the switchblade between his thumb and fingers. Daddy sat up straight. Trembling hands grasped the table. The breath caught in my throat as the man touched the sharp-pointed tip to Patricia's neck.

"Am I correct?" He tilted his head back, seeming to smile down the tip of his nose at Daddy and me. "We're not going to get up, are we, boys?"

In tiny jerks my head moved back and forth. Daddy's knuckles were white from gripping the table. Slowly, obediently, he made himself relax. He sank back in his chair and didn't move. He didn't even breathe.

The dark-complected man smiled again.

"That's good." His sleepy eyes left Daddy and me, to look up at the three men. "There's another boy. Find him!"

I heard the movement behind me, but I couldn't take my eyes from the sharp, silver blade at Patricia's throat.

"Ratcliff, Tubby," a calm voice called. "You go up. I'll check down here."

Footsteps pounded on the stairs. I could hear men walking above our heads. They scurried about the house. There were clunking sounds, thuds as doors opened and closed. My eyes were riveted to the knife. I hardly noticed when the men returned.

"No sign of him, Rico."

The man turned his sleepy eyes on my daddy. "Where's the boy?"

Daddy didn't move.

The knife that the man called Rico held so casually was still near Patricia's throat. Without taking his eyes from Daddy, the knife moved closer. The skin right beneath Patricia's jawbone dented with the pressure from the tip of the blade. My mouth opened. A small drop of blood trickled. It rolled down the shining, silver blade. The tiny gasp of air I took only went halfway down my throat before it stopped.

"I don't like to ask twice," Rico said.

Instantly, Daddy's hands sprang from the table. He waved them frantically.

"Okay. Okay. Don't hurt her, I'll—"

But before Daddy could finish:

"He's not here," Patricia lied. "He's spending the night with a friend."

Rico moved the knife away, just a fraction, and frowned.

"Why?"

Patricia blinked, then her eyes seemed to grow wide. "He . . . ah . . ."

"He and Sam got in a fight," Daddy said, speaking up quickly to help her out.

Rico stared down his nose at Daddy. He seemed

suspicious. He looked at Patricia the same way, then finally turned to glare at me.

"What was the fight about?"

"Ah . . . we . . . er, ah . . ." I stammered. I didn't know why Patricia and Daddy were lying—not for sure. But I had to go along with them. "We got in a fight over fishing. I . . . I didn't like taking the fish off the hook and it made him mad and—"

"Where did he go?" The man's voice was loud and mean.

Frantically, I tried to remember the names of the two friends Gary had mentioned just yesterday. It seemed like I sat there for an eternity, my heart throbbing in my ears.

"Robert. Robert, somebody. I don't know his last name. Honest."

"Robert Wimberly," Daddy continued. "Robert and his folks live about a mile from here. Gary walked over right before it got dark. He'll be back tomorrow evening."

Rico motioned to the phone on the kitchen wall. "Benny, see if there's a Wimberly in that book by the phone."

The man with the steel-gray eyes who had dragged me downstairs strolled over to the little table where the phone book was. He opened it. "Written in pencil, here on the front page," he answered. "Looks like a kid's handwriting."

I wanted to slump back in my chair—let out a huge

sigh of relief. But I forced myself to stay completely still.

The dark brows above Rico's sleepy eyes arched. The lie had worked. The men didn't know about Gary.

Maybe Gary had heard them drive up. Maybe he saw what happened. Maybe he knew they had hurt Daddy and Patricia and had run to get help. Or maybe . . .

"Tubby, you and Ratcliff check outside," Rico ordered. "Benny. Go check the barn."

Or maybe Gary was already sound asleep and hadn't heard a darned thing.

CHAPTER 16

I knew they were going to discover Gary. The thoughts raced so fast and furious through my brain, I couldn't keep track of them. There was no controlling the thoughts, either. They bounced from one thing to another.

If he had seen them drive up, he would have come to the house. But if he came just as they were breaking in and they hadn't seen him . . . No. If he had seen the two men grab Daddy, he would have tried to help. He would have rushed in, hitting and swinging and . . . Why did the man called Rico look so familiar? Had I seen him before? Why were they here? What did they want? Maybe Gary had gone for help. Why did they want to hurt us? Were they really going to hurt us? Were they planning to kill us? Maybe Gary had heard them and seen what was happening and was smart enough to know that he was just a kid and wouldn't stand a chance. If he was asleep in the barn—even if he was awake and hiding—the man they called Benny would find him and—

"Chicken's burning." Rico's voice snapped me from my frantic thoughts.

"Huh?"

Rico moved the knife from Patricia's throat and motioned with the tip toward the range. "Your chicken's burning." His eyes narrowed as he glanced down at his watch, then looked across the table at Daddy. "Ten-fifteen's a little late for supper, ain't it?"

Daddy didn't answer.

With a jerk of his head, Rico motioned to the frying pan. "I'll let you go ahead and finish cooking supper." He twirled the knife between his fingers. "So long as you both understand that I can reach the boy from here."

Patricia and Daddy nodded.

"Why are you here?" Daddy asked. "What do you want with us?"

Patricia got up cautiously and went to the range. Rico didn't answer. Patricia turned the chicken over with a long fork. For an instant I saw her eyes dart from the fork to the back of the man's head. Then she looked at me. Patricia clamped her lips together, put the fork on the counter and turned the range down.

"Why?" Daddy pleaded.

"We'll get to it, in time," Rico said, cleaning his fingernails with the switchblade. "Just know that if you cooperate, we won't be here long. You don't cooperate, there's gonna be more sufferin' and pain than you can imagine."

The way he said that left a chill down deep in my spine. I wiggled in the chair.

"You're going to kill us, aren't you?" Patricia asked flatly.

Rico tilted his head back and sneered down his nose at her. He didn't answer.

It was the way he looked at her—the way he *didn't answer*—that really scared me. The little chill that settled down deep in my spine was *nothing* compared to the cold that swept through me when Rico looked at Patricia.

My stomach rolled. I felt dizzy. I might have even passed out if it hadn't been for the sound of the front screen bouncing shut.

"Barn is clear," the one called Benny announced. "No sign of anybody."

The big man named Ratcliff and the tall, slender man named Tubby came back to the house shortly after Benny returned. They had seen nothing, either.

"Now will you tell us what you want?" Daddy asked.

Rico sneered down his nose at him. He almost laughed. "Soon as we eat supper."

They made Daddy and me sit on the floor by the wall, so Ratcliff, Benny, and Tubby could sit in our chairs. Patricia had to serve them *our* fried chicken and mashed potatoes. Rico told Patricia to pour him some iced tea. While he drank, he never took his sleepy eyes off us. The other three slopped down our food with the manners of hogs at a trough.

Once they finished, Rico ordered us back to the chairs. Ratcliff and Tubby tied Daddy's hands and feet to the rungs. Benny tied me, then Patricia.

"Sorry if it's too tight," he whispered, making sure the others didn't hear. "I hope I'm not hurting you."

I didn't respond.

Rico strolled casually to the kitchen cabinet. "Now then . . ." he said. Picking up a black leather case with a strap on it, he tossed it on the table. "Where's the picture?"

Daddy frowned. Patricia's brow wrinkled. I felt a little jerk. My hands trembled. It was my camera and case. No wonder I hadn't been able to find it when I packed. What did they want with my camera? What picture? I looked at the camera. I looked at Rico. He stared down his nose and his smile widened.

"Where's the picture?" he repeated.

My mouth flopped opened. I could feel my heart pounding in my ears.

He was the man . . . the two Learjets on the runway at the White Plains airport . . . the dark complexion, the sleepy eyes . . . the way he sneered down his nose when he spotted me. Rico was the man I had seen at the airport. The man who had raced inside after I'd taken the picture. He was the man who set off the metal detector—the one I thought was trying to catch a flight. Rico had been chasing *me*. He wanted the camera—the picture. Why?

Still frowning, Daddy shook his head.

"What picture?"

With her arms tied to the chair behind her, the little shrug Patricia gave was almost imperceptible.

"We don't know what picture you want."

Rico turned his sleepy eyes on me.

"The boy knows. Where is it?"

I made a little gulping sound when I swallowed. I could hardly breathe.

"It's—"

"Don't tell him!" Daddy's urgent shout cut me off. "Whatever they want—once they find it, they won't need us anymore. They'll—"

Ratcliff's huge fist cut him off. I heard the big hand slam against the side of Daddy's face. His chair tipped. I gasped. Daddy and the chair toppled over.

Patricia screamed. I felt the ropes bite into my wrists when I tried to jerk free. My chair scooted, but I couldn't move. Tied securely to the chair, Daddy was lying on his side. He twisted his neck so he could look up at me.

"Don't tell them," he moaned. "If they find what they want, they'll kill us. Don't—"

Ratcliff kicked my daddy. His foot drove deep into Daddy's side. I heard a cracking sound. Daddy coughed. Ratcliff kicked him again.

"Stop!" Patricia screamed. "Don't hurt him! Stop! Please stop!"

Ratcliff started to kick again, but Rico snapped his fingers. The big man stopped and looked back at Rico.

His leg was still back—cocked like the hammer of a gun.

Rico glared at me with those sleazy eyes.

"Where is it?"

I couldn't answer. With a quick jerk of his head, Rico motioned to Ratcliff. The foot slammed into my daddy again.

"It's in the darkroom!" I screamed. "The building by the barn. Don't kick him again. Don't hurt my daddy."

Rico's eyes scrunched down tight. "Where in the darkroom?"

"A fishbowl. It's the roll of film, right on top."

Rico smiled. He glanced down at Daddy, then at Ratcliff and Benny, and gave a little jerk of his head. That's all it took. They lifted Daddy and his chair and set him back by the table. Blood came from my daddy's cheek, where Ratcliff had hit him with his fist. I could hear him wheeze, trying to catch his breath.

The tall skinny man named Tubby moved to stand above me. When he leaned to smile down at me, he traced his tongue over his paper-thin lips.

"Little boys should always listen to their dads." He laughed. "You done went and killed your whole family, boy. Shoulda kept your mouth shut."

CHAPTER 17

hat's enough!" Benny's steel-gray eyes cut through Tubby like he was no more than a spoonful of whipped cream. "Shut up."

Tubby obeyed. His skinny frame slumped and he slinked back into the corner by the fridge.

Ratcliff moved toward the table. "Come on, Rico. Let's do 'em and get out of here."

Rico sneered at him. "You and Benny go check the darkroom." He looked down his nose at me. "The film developed?"

I shook my head.

He said a bad word and turned to Tubby. "Call New York and get Alex on the phone. They'll have to fly someone down to develop the film. We got to make sure we got the right one—the right picture before . . ." He paused long enough to look at us. ". . . before we're done here."

Tubby started for the phone. Rico jerked his head

toward the living room. "Use the other phone. Don't want these nice folks trying to yell at the operator or anything like that. And use the car phone. We don't want the number traced here. Benny, Ratcliff, go get the film."

I felt the tears leak from my eyes.

"It's all right," Patricia said soothingly. "You were just trying to protect your dad. It's all right. Sam."

"Shut up!" Rico snapped. Then more calmly: "Just sit still and keep your mouth shut."

I had sniffed and sniffed and finally stopped crying by the time Ratcliff burst back into the kitchen. He marched straight for me. His big fist grabbed the front of my shirt and he lifted me and the chair I was tied to clear off the ground.

"Where did you say the film was?" he snarled.

"The fishbowl." I blinked. "It's the roll right on the top."

He dropped me and the chair. Quietly, he spun to face Rico. "We got a problem, boss. You better come take a look."

Rico tested the ropes that held Patricia, Daddy, and me. Then he scurried off on Ratcliff's heels. In the other room I could hear Tubby's voice. I couldn't tell what he was saying, though.

"I didn't mean to tell, Daddy," I whispered. "I'm sorry. They were hurting you and—"

There was a creaking sound. A board squeaked. Without turning our heads, all three of us glanced toward the back door.

Gary was there. Crouched down, he sneaked through the doorway. He let the door shut without a sound then dropped to his hands and knees. Quick as a cat, he crawled across the floor.

I leaned to the side, listening. I could still hear Tubby. Gary scurried to Daddy's chair. Frantic fingers began working on the ropes. Within moments Daddy was free. He slipped from his chair, paused a second to listen for Tubby's voice on the phone, then began to untie me. The ropes dropped loose from around my hands. I wiggled my wrists. It felt good. Then as Gary and I begun untying the ropes around my ankles, Daddy slid over to Patricia. He paused, once more to make sure Tubby was still talking.

"These guys are professionals," he whispered as Gary and I crept over to help loosen Patricia's ropes. "They don't want to leave any witnesses. Do you two . . ." He paused, holding his breath to listen. All of us froze. Tubby was still talking. ". . . understand? Do you understand that they're planning to kill us?"

Gary and I nodded.

The knot at Patricia's ankle was hard as a rock. I dug and dug at it with my fingernails. Finally, I wedged a finger under it and pulled the rope through one of the loops.

"You've got to get out of here and get help." Daddy's voice was no louder than a soft breeze. "If anything happens and we get separated"—he paused again to listen—"don't come back. Get the police or—"

The front screen slammed shut. Daddy's head jerked up like a cork popping from a champagne bottle. Voices, sharp and gruff, boomed from the other room. Patricia's hands were loose. She brushed my fingers away from the knot and began working on it herself.

"They're coming." Daddy breathed out loud. "Go! Get out!"

Patricia shoved me toward the door. Daddy pushed Gary toward me and sprang to his feet. "I'll slow 'em down. Get out!" His voice was no longer a whisper.

"RUN!" He screamed.

Daddy charged for the doorway to hold the men and cover our escape. As Gary and I raced for the back door, I could hear him roar from behind us:

"No matter what happens. No matter what they say or do—*don't stop!* Don't come back! *Run!*"

"Don't stop!" Patricia echoed. *"Run!"*

CHAPTER 18

The sounds from the house were horrid. I could hear furniture crashing, things breaking, shouts and curses.

Gary burst through the back door. I was so close behind him the screen didn't have time to bounce shut before I slipped through, hot on his heels. He jumped from the porch and sprinted to the left. In the glow from the lights in the house, I could see the ground. I raced after him.

Just before he made it to the rocks at the left side of the cliff, I heard Patricia scream. Without breaking stride I glanced over my shoulder.

She'd gotten her ropes loose and was at the back door. One of the men had hold of her. She clung to the doorjamb with both hands, kicking and struggling. She couldn't get away, but at the same instant I realized that, I understood that the man who had hold of her couldn't get free, either. The longer she held onto the doorjamb, the more head start she was buying for

Gary and me. Gary leaped from one rock down to another and then another. I followed.

Suddenly I stopped. Without the light from the house, the darkness below me was like a bottomless pit. The moon was no more than a silver half-crescent in the sky. Below, there was nothing but black.

"Come on," Gary urged in a whisper.

"I can't," I whispered back. I could hear the shouts and scuffling from the house. "I can't see."

Gary grabbed my wrist. He tugged, but my feet were frozen to the rock.

"I can't," I repeated.

He yanked. "Jump where I jump. Come on. Your eyes will get used to it in a minute."

Gary leaped for the next rock. As soon as he landed, he tugged my arm and I jumped. He caught me each time. Held me until I had my balance, then hopped to the next boulder.

"Which way did they go?" Rico screeched from behind us.

"Don't know. Didn't see 'em." The others answered in unison.

"Tubby!" Rico's voice boomed. "Head toward the barn and the shed. Ratcliff, circle 'round front of the house. See if they went that way. I'll check the cliff."

Gary jumped again. Caught me when I landed. Then again and a third time. This time he didn't let go. Both of us stood still. We hugged each other and looked up.

Rico stood on the ledge, not thirty feet above us.

With the light behind him, I couldn't see his eyes. All I could see was his shape outlined by the light from the house as he raised his arm. A glimmer of light caught an object in his hand. It was a gun barrel. Gary and I clung tighter. Like two monkeys just released into a zoo cage, we hugged and wrapped ourselves around each other as if our lives depended on it.

Rico was looking straight at us. He aimed the gun.

I closed my eyes. "Please don't let it hurt," I prayed. "Please make it be quick."

Not breathing, not moving, Gary and I hugged each other for what seemed an eternity. The sound of a gunshot didn't come. I cracked one eye open. Rico, still leaning over the cliff and still aiming the pistol, moved to the right. He followed the rim of the canyon—away from us. A sigh slipped from my throat. Gary held me tightly.

"He can't see us," Gary whispered. His lips were so close they brushed the little hairs on my ear. "He don't know where the rock slide is. Soon as he moves off a bit, where he can't hear, we'll go on down."

Nervously, we waited as Rico followed the lip of the canyon rim. He moved farther and farther to the right.

"Now," Gary urged. He jumped to the next rock and tugged me after him. Silently, swiftly, we began to work our way down.

"Didn't hear or see nothin' in the barn, boss. They could be holed up in there. So dark, I can't tell."

I just landed on the rock with Gary when Ratcliff's voice echoed from above us. Gary made sure I had my balance and was just loosening his grip to jump again. Instead he hugged me and held tight. We both looked up.

Far above and to the side of where we stood, I could see the two men silhouetted on the edge of the cliff. Again we held our breath. Didn't move. Didn't make a sound.

"Tubby?" Rico's voice bounced back at us from the far side of the canyon.

"Nothin' out front, boss." Tubby's voice was far away and muffled. "So dark, I can't see nothin'."

I blinked a couple of times and looked around. The light from the moon wasn't much, but I could see the shape of rocks. What if . . .

I leaned close to Gary's ear. "I can see," I whispered. "My eyes adjusted, like you said. What if the men can—"

Gary shook his head, cutting me off. He moved his face so he could lean closer to my ear.

"We're too far down. They can't see this far as dark as it is. We're safe so long as we don't make any noise."

"Tubby," Rico called. "Get in the trunk and break out the night-vision glasses. Hurry!"

CHAPTER 19

Gary practically dragged me off my feet. He jumped to the next rock. Then jerking me along with him, he leaped to the next. I teetered, lost my balance. He caught me.

"Hurry," he whispered. "We've only got a couple of minutes."

As we moved I noticed that we were no longer making our way down the rock slide. Instead we were moving toward the side—toward the sheer rock cliff.

"Why aren't we going down? This isn't the way. We have to—"

"Shut up and move!" His whisper was sharp and urgent.

Although I couldn't see that far, my guess was that we were still twenty yards or so above the canyon floor when Gary stopped. We teetered on a big boulder near the sheer rock cliff. He pushed me in front of him to a narrow, granite outcropping. Quickly, he moved beside me and flattened his back against the bare stone.

I stood there only a second before leaning forward so I could see Rico.

"What's night-vision glasses? Why did we stop?"

Gary reached out and shoved me back against the cold rock.

"They're things the army uses so they can see in the dark. My friend's dad has a pair. You can see like it's daytime with those things. They see us out in the open and we're as good as—"

"You boys stop, right where you are," Rico yelled from above us. "I can see you. You take another step and I'll shoot."

We held our breath and pressed harder against the smooth rock.

"I mean it! I'll shoot!"

There was a loud pop. It didn't sound like the gunshots I heard on TV westerns or cop shows. The sound was more like a cap gun. A high-pitched zing pierced the night air. Rico shot again.

"He can't see us," Gary breathed. "He's just shootin'. Not even coming close. He's bluffin'."

There was a long silence. Rico was waiting—trying to flush us out.

Gary smiled. "See, he ain't got no idea where we went."

The silence was deafening. Nothing broke the stillness. We waited.

"All right. You've got thirty seconds to show yourselves. I mean it!" Rico's angry voice shook the night. "You don't show yourself in thirty seconds . . . I'm gonna kill your folks."

The silence fell once more. My heart must have stopped because I couldn't even hear it pounding in my chest. There was only the ominous stillness.

"I'm not kiddin'. You got twenty seconds."

My legs began to shake. I forced them to stop, but as soon as I did, my hands started to tremble. I grabbed my thighs and squeezed tight.

"Ten seconds or they're *dead!*"

Gary took a deep breath. His shoulders slumped as he leaned forward. He took a step toward the rock slide where we had climbed down.

My arm sprang out as quick as the flick of a snake's tongue. I grabbed his shirt, pulled him back, and at the same time slammed him against the rock.

"No!" I whispered.

"He's gonna kill 'em." Gary's voice was almost a whisper. "We got to—"

"No," I repeated. "Remember what Dad and your mom told us? 'Don't come back. No matter what they say or do . . . don't come back.' Remember?"

He nodded.

"I told them where the film was." I sighed. "Daddy told me not to, but I told them, anyway. I won't make the same mistake again. This time, I'm going to do *exactly* what Daddy said—no matter what."

Again we fell silent. Waited. Inside my head, I counted—one thousand one, one thousand two, one thousand three ... After thirty seconds there was still nothing but quiet. No gunshot. No scream. Just the empty, frightening silence.

Voices came once more. The words weren't yelled or shouted this time. Instead the men talked so softly, I could only make out a word or two every now and then.

"Car and check the roads ... circle out here ... see if ... path going down ... call ... send more men to find ... If ... then shoot ... stupid boys ... can't afford to let them ..."

The voices faded as the men moved away from the edge of the cliff. Gary leaned toward me.

"We got to move. We gotta get help."

I pointed up at the cliff. "But those glasses. Those night things. What if ..."

The moonlight caught Gary's teeth as he bit his bottom lip. He looked back at the rock slide then down.

"Can't go back to the rocks," he said. "Too open. We'll have to go down the cliff. When we reach the bottom, if we stay close enough to it, they won't be able to see. Come on."

Gary turned to face the sheer rock wall. He eased himself down until his knees rested on the little ledge where we stood. Then using his hands, he lowered himself over the edge.

"Too dark to see," he whispered. "Use your feet and hands to feel for holds before you let go of anything."

I turned around to face the cliff. Clinging to the

bare rock with my hands, I knelt and lowered myself as Gary had done.

I had thought that hopping from rock to rock in the dark was hard work. Making our way down the straight rock cliff would be impossible. I'd seen the cliff the day Gary pretended to fall when we were playing soccer. It was a fifty-foot drop from the top— nothing but smooth rock, as slick as a pane of glass. But as we started down, I found that it wasn't as impossible as I had imagined.

There were little knobs of stone that protruded from the cliff, just big enough to catch under my tennis shoe and support my weight. There were cracks and crevices, wide enough to wedge the toe of my tennis shoe in or wiggle my fingers into so I could hang on. Side by side, an inch at a time, we worked our way down the cliff.

Yesterday when we went fishing, it had only taken forty-five minutes to follow the rock slide to the canyon floor. In the dark, moving an inch at a time, searching for handholds or tiny pieces of rock to wrap the toe of my tennis shoe around, it took us more than three times that long. Fact was, it took forever to reach the bottom. Once there, the going was still pretty tough. We had to stay close to the edge of the rock wall to keep from being seen from above. The ground was strewn with loose rock and rubble that had fallen from the cliff. It was hard to walk and keep our balance, much less move quietly so we wouldn't be heard.

The half-moon was straight overhead when we came to a sharp bend in the cliff. The wall curved to the right and went upward where a small stream flowed down to join the one that trickled through the center of the valley.

"We're right under where the barn and darkroom are," Gary whispered. He was panting and out of breath like I was.

"Is this where we go back up?"

Gary shook his head. "No. We follow that little valley, it'd take us to the road, but if they're out in the car, looking for us, we'd be too easy to spot."

"So, what do we do?"

"So," he said pointing to the stream. "Remember that place where we went fishin'?"

"Yes."

" 'Bout a mile or so past that sandbar is Robinson's Landing."

"What's that?"

"It's a boat dock. There's a café and a bunch of houses and stuff around. Figure if we make it there, we could find a phone or get to somebody's house and call the cops."

I nodded my agreement and started toward the stream.

Gary stopped me. "We're gonna have to make it across this open ground first. It's about a hundred yards before the stream bends and we're outta sight again. I'll go first. I'll get to that tree, yonder." He pointed to a little scrub oak that was gnarled and bent. "There's a yard light up by the barn. I'll be able to see 'em. If it's clear, I'll wave for you to come on. You wait here till I wave, got it?"

I leaned back against the rock. Gary took a couple of deep breaths, then sprinted for the oak tree. I waited. It was the first time I'd had a chance to stop and rest since the men broke into the house. I took a deep breath and tried to make myself relax. My feet ached and throbbed from where my new tennis shoes rubbed them. The tips of my fingers felt red-hot from wedging them into the rocks when we worked our way down the cliff.

Gary raced for the tree. When he reached it, he slid, like a baseball player sliding into second base. I could hardly see him. Finally he rose up on his knees and waved to me.

I took a deep breath and charged toward him. I'd only taken two or three strides when he began frantically waving both arms. I didn't even have time to stop before I heard the voices:

"There they are!"

"Where?"

"Under that tree."

"Where's the other one?"

"There he is. Running. Shoot 'em! Shoot 'em both!"

CHAPTER 20

I'd never been shot at before. I didn't like it!

How many popgunlike shots there were, I had no idea. I was too scared and running too hard to count. I hated the whiz and zing as the bullets cut the night air. I wanted to scream when I heard the pieces of lead rip through tree limbs or branches, and the crack when they slammed against a rock.

The brush tore at my bare arms and caught my shirt. I kept running. I fell, but scrambled to my feet and charged blindly into the night. Running—running for my life.

We were probably a quarter of a mile down the stream before we stopped. Gary fell first. He crumpled to the ground, gasping for air. I collapsed beside him. My sides hurt so much I could barely breathe. I thought I was going to die.

My arms felt like strands of limp spaghetti. I could

hardly lift them. Still, I did. I slugged Gary smack in the stomach.

"You almost got me killed," I gasped.

I heard a little snort as he doubled up and held his stomach where I'd punched him.

"Hey," he moaned.

"You almost got me killed," I repeated.

We lay for a while, gasping for air and trying to catch our breath. Finally Gary sat up.

"I didn't see 'em." He shook his head. "They were sittin' on the edge of the cliff in the shadow of the barn. I didn't even see 'em till they stood up and started shootin'."

I panted awhile longer, until I was able to sit up beside him. Gary got real still. He looked at me for a long moment, then he hit me. He slugged me, hard as he could, on the arm.

I jerked and rubbed my arm. "Hey, what was that for?"

He glared at me. "You hit me for almost getting us killed. You're the one who almost got us killed. It's all your fault."

"My fault!" My voice squeaked.

"Yeah. They're after some picture you took. Why? What did you take a picture of?"

I shook my head. "I don't know. There were a couple of airplanes and—"

Suddenly Gary was on his feet in front of me. He grabbed my T-shirt and practically yanked me off the ground.

"You take a picture of one of those guys killing somebody? Selling drugs? What was it?"

With a swing of my arm, I knocked his hands away from my shirt.

"I don't know!" Then softer, feeling totally helpless and confused, I whispered, "Honest. At the airport in White Plains, I remember seeing that Rico guy. There were two Learjets. There were some men standing around, and he was one of them. I was just shooting some pictures so Daddy wouldn't be disappointed that I hadn't been using the camera he gave me. That's all. I don't know what they want. Honest to God I don't."

Gary glared at me for a long time. Finally his shoulders drooped. He spun and plopped back to the ground.

"So, what now?" I asked, glancing back toward the cliff. "Are they following us? Are they coming after us?"

"You can bet on it." Gary nodded. "It's gonna take 'em a while to get down the cliff. Even with them night-vision glasses, they don't know the path. But they'll be coming. You ready? Can you move yet?"

My knee throbbed. I remembered falling a couple of times when we ran. I didn't feel the pain until now. I rubbed my knee and felt the damp spot where blood had leaked through my blue jeans. My arms stung from all the branches that had scraped my skin.

"You okay? You ready to get goin'?" Gary repeated when I didn't answer.

I shook my head. "I'm not okay, but let's go." I reached out and helped him to his feet.

Limping behind, I followed Gary along the stream bank. We were well past the curve in the valley that took us out of sight from the cliff. We stayed in the open so we could move faster. My tennis shoes rubbed at the blisters on my heels with each step. Every time my right foot came down, pain shot from my knee clear up into my skull. I kept walking.

Three hours, maybe four—I had no idea how long we walked, stumbled, fell, climbed to our feet, only to stumble and fall again. The sky was lighter now, the moon not so bright. On the horizon, clouds that had looked white with the glow from the moon now turned a deep purple. The next time I glanced up, bright pinks and oranges seemed to blend in with the purple. The trees on the hills and ridges started to show a faint tint of green. I could see the little stream, instead of just hearing it gurgle as we moved beside it. The sky slowly became a bright orange, streaked with every color under the rainbow. Despite my fear and panic, I couldn't help notice how beautiful the sunrise was.

"Sky sure is pretty," I mentioned, wanting Gary to notice.

He didn't even look up. "It's pretty, all right, but don't be lookin' at the sky. This is the time a day the rattles come out. You best watch where you're steppin'."

It was almost light when we came around a rock

knoll. In the distance I could see the little sandbar where Gary and I had fished. I could see the tall cliff that stood above it, forcing the river into a narrow channel.

We were almost there. A smile tugged at the corners of my face. What had Gary said: Robinson's Landing was only a mile or so from the sandbar. We made it. We could call for help. We were safe and—

All at once Gary stopped. I started to take another step, but before my foot came down he spun around and dove at me. Like a linebacker sacking a quarterback, one second he stood facing me, the next his shoulder and arm were driven into my stomach. They knocked the air from me. I doubled over as the force of his tackle threw me to the ground. A rock dug at my left shoulder blade.

My mouth opened to scream. No sound came out. In a flash Gary had crawled up my stomach and chest. He'd clamped a hand over my mouth before any sound could escape. Eyes wide in shock, I stared at him. With a jerk of his head, he motioned toward the sandbar. I closed my mouth and pulled my face away from his hand. I looked where he was motioning but couldn't see anything. He jerked his head again and eased his weight off me.

On our hands and knees we crawled to the rock knoll. I rose up to peek over one of the stones. My eyes flashed again.

Standing on the cliff that overlooked the sandbar was the one called Tubby.

Instinct made me duck behind the rock. After a second I cautiously rose again. In the half-light of dawn it was hard to see the details. I could tell it was Tubby from his tall, skinny build. He had something on his head, on his face. I squinted, trying to see what it was. It looked like binoculars, only flatter and smaller. A dark strap held them to his head.

I crouched behind the rock and looked at Gary.

"Those the night-vision glasses he has on?"

Gary nodded and we both peeked up to watch him again. Tubby took the glasses from his head. Then he put them back on, then took them off once more.

"The dawn light is messin' him up," Gary whispered. "He can't tell whether he can see better with 'em or without 'em this time of day."

"Can we slip past him?"

Gary shook his head, then slumped back against a rock. He tucked his knees up and held them tight against his chest. Frowning, as if in deep thought, he rocked back and forth.

I pointed to the right.

"What's that way?"

"Road's about a mile off. No houses on that section. Closest ones are about two miles on over. But if they're driving around on the roads, watching for us . . ."

I motioned to the left. "What about that way?"

Gary sighed. "That's the Refuge. Six . . . maybe eight miles to the road. Rough as the ground is, it'd take us a day or more just to make the pavement. There aren't any houses, either. Fort Sill is the other side of the road, but it's the West Range. Don't get to any army housing for another six to eight miles. Mom and Dad need help. That way'd take us forever."

Making sure I was hidden from Tubby behind the rock, I eased to my feet.

"What if we go back the way we came?"

Gary blinked. "Can't. We'd have to go under the cliff."

"It's daylight," I said. "We can see them as well as they can see us. We can make sure they're not watching and stay close to the cliff. Is there anyplace we can get help if we get past the house?"

Gary nodded. "Mrs. Brooks lives about a mile up the canyon from us. Her home's way back off the road. They might not be watching there."

Stooped low, we crept back the way we had come. Once well-concealed beyond the rock knoll, we straightened and were able to walk faster. We had only gone about a hundred yards or so when we heard something.

Both of us stopped, listening.

A dry stream bed trailed up into the rocks on our right. The sound didn't come from there. I tilted my head, trying to make out the noise and determine where it was coming from.

Branches and dead twigs snapped. There was a whacking sound, like sticks slapping together. The noise grew closer. I could hear talking now. But only one voice. Foul, nasty words shouted into the once beautiful light of early morning. Far up the canyon I caught a movement. I glimpsed a white T-shirt. Even at this distance I could make out the big, lumpy, muscled arm that came from the shirt sleeve.

Ratcliff—the big, ugly monster—was coming straight for us.

CHAPTER 21

"What can we do?" I whispered close to Gary's ear.

Gary didn't answer. I nudged him with my elbow.

"What?"

Gary shook his head. "We're caught. There's nothin' we can do. I've done everything I know to do. There's no place left to go."

"We got to do something," I protested.

"We're caught. They're gonna kill us and Mama and Daddy and . . . there's nothing left for us to do."

Gary had been the leader. He'd helped me down the rock slide. He'd led as we climbed down the sheer rock cliff. He'd gotten us away from the bullets that cut through the still night air.

Now, Gary stood stooped and helpless. His arms dangled limp at his sides. He didn't even look toward Ratcliff as the huge, ugly man crashed through the brush, closer and closer with each step. Gary stood, waiting like a mouse caught in one of those glue traps.

Waiting and resigned to his fate. He'd brought us so far, but now he'd given up.

I glanced at the dry creek bed on our right. I grabbed Gary's wrist and yanked with all my might. Off balance, staggering and stumbling, Gary dragged along behind me as I charged up the creek bed. We'd gone only about fifty yards—still in plain sight of the canyon where Ratcliff was walking—when a rock cliff blocked our path. It was like a box canyon that cowboys talk about on reruns of old TV westerns. Three sides went straight up. Three walls of bare rock closed us in. The only escape was back the way we had come. Back toward the big man with the white T-shirt.

Frantically, I searched around. To the side was a big gap or crevice in the rock. Gary stood waiting for the end, but I grabbed his shoulders and shoved him into the crack in the rock. Then, shoving and bumping and wiggling, I squeezed in next to him.

Ratcliff's voice was louder. I could see the canyon, and I knew that if he glanced in this direction, he could see me as well. At the first glimpse of the white T-shirt, I held my breath. Didn't move.

The man cursed and yelled. He had a heavy stick in his right hand, a walkie-talkie in his left. He cursed and shouted and pounded the brush with the stick.

I leaned toward Gary.

"He's trying to drive us down to Tubby," I said in a whisper. "They're trying to trap us between them. That's why he's making so much noise."

Gary didn't respond. He only stared blankly at the rock in front of his nose.

That's when I saw the tracks we'd left. There were little depressions in the sand at the bottom of the dry creek bed that we'd followed. The tracks in the sand led right to where Gary and I were hiding in the rock crevice. I swallowed, but my mouth was dry and my tongue stuck to the back of my throat. One glance was all it would take. If he so much as looked down at the sand . . .

Ratcliff, still roaring like an angry bear and beating the bushes with his stick, walked right past the streambed.

We waited until he was well out of sight and his voice began to fade. Then, with me shoving Gary, we made our way up the crevice to the top of the box canyon. It was a steep, hard climb. By the time we reached the top, I was exhausted. All I wanted to do was curl up on a rock and sleep.

Gary came alive again. "Come on," he urged. "We gotta make some time."

"Just a minute," I pleaded. "I have to catch my breath."

He tugged at my arm. "We don't have a minute. Soon as Ratcliff makes it down to where Tubby is, they'll figure out they missed us. They'll start back-tracking. It won't be hard for even city guys to find our trail . . . in . . . the . . ." Gary's voice faded with each word. I couldn't help but notice the smile that came to his face as he glanced around. "Stay here," he said, almost laughing. "Don't move."

There was another dry streambed, near us at the top of the canyon. It wound its way down from the mountains to disappear over a sharp, rock outcropping at the edge of the cliff we had just climbed. Probably, after a heavy rain, there was a pretty waterfall there that filled the dry streambed below. Quickly, leaping from one rock to the next, Gary made his way to the streambed. He hopped into the middle of the dry streambed and started walking. Well, he really wasn't walking, he was stomping. Each step he took, his foot pounded deep into the sand. After some twenty to thirty feet he left the creek bed and hopped to a big boulder. Bounding from one rock to the next, he circled back to where he'd left me.

"City folks don't know dip about trackin'." He grinned. "See them tracks? They'll see 'em and just know we went up the creek. Only we're going this way." He pointed toward a small peak to our left. "Come on. Stay on the rocks. Just the rocks! Don't let your feet hit the ground till we've gone about a hundred yards or so."

I followed Gary, but not for very long before I stopped him. "We can't go this way." I tugged at his shirtsleeve. "You said it was between six and eight miles to the road, and if we didn't find help there, it was another eight miles across Fort Sill. We don't have that much time."

Frowning, he turned to look at me.

"Huh?"

"We don't have time," I repeated. "They know where the film is. Soon as they're sure they've got the right picture—the one they're looking for—they won't have any need for Patricia and . . . and Daddy . . . and they'll . . ."

"They ain't gonna find the film." Gary's face seemed to glow with that sloppy smile of his.

"They're not?"

He shook his head. "I sneaked up to the kitchen window when they were talkin'. Soon as I heard you blab about where the film was, I ran to the shed and took care of it."

"How?"

"Easy." He shrugged. "You know the fishbowl?"

I nodded.

"Dumped the whole thing on the floor." Gary almost laughed. "There's probably fifty rolls of film in that thing. Gonna take 'em forever to go through it."

I felt my eyes tighten. "What if they get lucky?"

"They won't. The film they're lookin' for ain't in there. I moved it."

"Where?"

Gary looked at me for a moment, then turned and walked away.

"Where?" I repeated.

"Ain't none of your business," he called over his shoulder. "Long as you don't know, you can't tell 'em nothin'. Now, come on . . ." Under his breath, he added, "Dumb city kid."

I hesitated a moment, glaring at the back of his head. In a way, I couldn't blame Gary for not confiding in me. In another way, what he said made me feel no bigger than a fly speck beneath his feet. I wanted to crumple up and sit down on one of the rocks—sit and pout like some little kid until he came back for me. I forced my feet to move. Feeling totally useless, I began to follow him.

CHAPTER 22

The Wichita Mountains were nothing like the Cat-skills. There were no nature trails. Fact was, there were no trials whatsoever. Each step was like trodding on land where no human had ever traveled before. The ground was rough and strewn with rocks.

The peak that Gary called Mount Scott towered above us on the left. In places, giant granite boulders seemed to flow down from the summit like rivers of rock. Oak trees were scattered around the sides, as if forming riverbanks to contain the unmoving flow. I found myself fascinated by the strange rustic beauty of this place. Had circumstances been differ-ent, I could have stayed and explored the majesty forever.

By midmorning my fascination began to wane. I could feel the beads of sweat popping out on my face. My shirt was damp. I'd never been in a place so hot. There was no wind, and even when we moved through the shadows of the little valleys, the heat seemed to wrap around me like a wet blanket. My shoes rubbed my heels.

By noon I couldn't take it anymore.

My feet hurt so badly that each step made me want to scream. My mouth felt like I'd eaten cotton balls. I couldn't even swallow. I could simply go no farther.

At the top of a little ridge ahead of me, Gary stopped and glanced back. For an instant he frowned when he saw I had collapsed on a rock. Then a little smile came to his face.

"Stream and a little pool, just the other side of this hill." He pointed. "Looks like there might even be a dewberry clump or somethin'. Come on."

I stared down at the ground and shook my head.

"I'm tired, too," he called. "But over yonder is a lot better place. It's just a little ways."

I shook my head. "I can't."

After a long moment I heard Gary sigh.

"Well, you go ahead and sit here in the sun. I'm goin' over in the shade and soak my feet in that cool water."

"Fine."

He folded his arms and took one more step away from where I sat.

"I always knew you were a wimp, *S-a-m-m-y.*"

He stretched my name out, like he knew how much I hated being called Sammy. Then, with that sloppy grin on his face, he turned and walked away.

"S-a-m-m-y Ross is nothin' but a pansy. Dumb city slicker."

It was the straw that broke the camel's back.

My weak legs popped like springs. I leaped to my feet and charged him like a grizzly bear. My hatred for this obnoxious hick was stronger than the pain from my blistered feet. It was more powerful than the fear and panic that had kept me going this far. Getting my hands on him—for just one second—was far more pressing and important than seeking help for Patricia and Daddy.

I'd had enough. I was going to kill Gary.

How he managed to stay barely out of my reach, I don't know. I chased after him, determined to rip him apart with my bare hands. I followed him over the ridge and down into the valley where the little stream was.

Once there, Gary collapsed on the bank beside a pool of still, clear water. I reached him, and for a second I thought about kicking him while he was lying there. Instead I flopped down beside him.

"Think you're pretty smart?" I huffed, trying to catch my breath. "Don't you?"

"Sorry," he panted back. "It worked, didn't it?"

Exhausted, we lay on our backs for a long time before we sat up and took off our shoes and socks.

"My gosh!" Gary gasped. "Ain't never seen blisters that bad before. Got a giant blister on each heel. Looks like they done busted and new ones has popped up underneath. How can you even walk on them things?"

The only thing I could do was shrug.

My feet were so hurt and hot, the water felt like ice when I eased them into the pool. I yanked them up and lowered them again. After a while Gary grunted and got to his feet.

"You ain't gonna be able to walk much farther with them blisters, less we do somethin'," he observed. "We'll figure out some way to fix you up, but first we got to cool down."

We stripped out of our clothes so they wouldn't get soaked and waded out into the little pool. The water was fresh and clear and cool. We swam and splashed. I had heard once that drinking the water from a pond or stream would make me sick. Still, I waded over to where the stream flowed into the pool and took a couple of mouthfuls. I sloshed it around and then spit it out. It helped get rid of the cotton in my mouth.

I felt almost alive again when we crawled out on the bank. I knew the feeling wouldn't last.

We dressed, except for our shoes and socks. Gary took both pairs of socks and went back to the water. He rubbed them again and again in the sand at the edge of the pool, then sloshed them about in clean water. Once satisfied that they were clean, he draped them over a bush, slipped his bare feet into his shoes, and went to inspect the berry patch.

"Birds already got all the ripe ones," he called. "Green ones would make us sick."

As he returned to where I lay, he reached in the right pocket of his jeans and pulled out a pocketknife. Then he dug in his left pocket until he produced a silver-colored tube, about three inches long.

"What's that?" I asked.

"Match holder. Keeps matches dry when you're out campin' and stuff. I don't never leave home without my pocketknife and matches."

I watched as he used his thumb to raise and extend one of the blades on his knife. He then unscrewed the end of the match holder and pulled out a long kitchen match. One side of the tube was rough, as if someone had attached a sharp-toothed fingernail file to the thing. Gary replaced the top and struck the match on the rough side. He waved the match back and forth under the tip of the knife, then blew it out and turned to me.

"Heist your foot up here. Let me fix'er for you."

My eyes almost bugged out of my head.

"Forget it," I yelped. "I ain't lettin' you get hold of me with that knife."

I blinked and felt my forehead wrinkle up with the realization that I was beginning to sound just like Gary. It was a horrible thought. I cleared my throat.

"I mean, I refuse to allow you to touch my foot."

He shrugged and handed me the knife.

"Fine. You do it."

Reluctantly, hands trembling, I eased the blade toward the heel of my foot.

"Go on," he encouraged. "Them things is puffed up tight as a balloon that's fixin' to pop. There's so much pressure, you won't even feel it."

Gary was right. The tip of the blade touched the clear, tightly stretched skin at the edge of the blister. The yucky, clear, oozy stuff poured out, and the only thing I felt was relief from the pounding, throbbing pressure. He took another match from the holder and sterilized the blade again. I did the same thing with the enormous blister on my other heel.

"It ain't gonna help all that much," he told me. "But it'll keep you goin' for a while."

He brought the socks back. They were dry.

"Put both pair on." Gary instructed. "It'll keep your shoes from rubbin' so bad."

"What about you?"

"Don't need 'em. These shoes is broke in right good. Come on. Get 'em on and let's get movin'."

Hour after endless hour we walked and walked and walked. For the first few minutes my heels didn't hurt. But soon enough, even with two pair of socks and lanced blisters, my feet started to throb and ache again.

We sweltered in the heat and the sticky humidity. Our stomachs growled, complaining about lack of food. Still, we kept walking.

Then I saw it. We topped a small knoll of rock, and

below I saw a road. The pavement looked like a silver ribbon, bright and shiny in the afternoon sunlight. We were so close, I could even see the yellow stripes down the center of the highway.

"Come on." Gary waved and began jogging down the slope toward the road. "We can find a Game Ranger or tourists—somebody to catch a ride with. Get help."

Each step was agony. My mouth was cotton-dry again. Still, I raced after him. The closer we got to the road, the less I noticed the pain. We were almost safe.

The road was empty. We stood in the center, right on top of the yellow stripes. We looked to the left then the right. There was nothing but ripples of heat rising from the hot, empty road.

"Where is everybody?" I gasped.

"It's a weekday," Gary answered. "Ain't much traffic during the week, mostly folks come out to watch the wildlife on the weekends."

I pointed to the left. "Maybe if we walk toward that mountain. The one with the road going up. Maybe we could—"

Suddenly, Gary waved.

"Shush. Listen!"

There was the sound of a motor. I tilted my head, first to one side then the other. The engine whined in the distance, but I couldn't tell from which direction the sound came.

"Where is it?"

Gary shushed me again.

Then to our left I saw a white pickup truck. It came around a curve and burst into view. It was going so fast, it fishtailed as it rounded the corner. And just as I saw it, I spotted the black sedan that was behind it.

"It's them," Gary screamed. *"Run!"*

CHAPTER 23

We had just bounded across the shallow ditch on the far side of the road when the sound of tires squealing screamed in my ears. I raced on. Following Gary, I dodged around oak trees, leaped over rocks, ducked and sprinted through the forest.

Behind me I heard car doors slamming.

I ran harder.

The voices and shouts were close at first. Branches snapping behind us sent chills scampering up my back. But the harder we ran, the more distance we covered and the more faint the sounds became.

Suddenly there was a fence. It looked like what Justin Porter called "hog-wire"—the kind of fence with which his dad had built the pen for their golden Lab. Only this fence was huge. The openings in the welded wire were almost a foot square. The wire itself was almost as big around as my little finger. The fence towered above us, suspended between twelve-foot-high poles.

Without hesitation, Gary leaped as high as he could. For an instant he hung there like a fly clinging to a screen window. Then he started to climb. I followed him.

"There . . ." a voice boomed in the distance.

It took forever to get over the huge fence. Once our feet hit the ground on the other side, we ran and ran and ran.

"Think we lost 'em?" I panted. The bare ground under my back was cool. Leaves on the tall oak tree swayed and jiggled with the soft breeze above where we lay.

"Don't know," Gary gasped back.

Then both of us gulped in big breaths of air, held them and listened. There was no sound of voices or shouts. There was no crack of dead tree branches snapping under running feet. There was only the slight rustle of the wind. Both of us panted and gasped for air once more.

When our sides finally quit throbbing with each beat of our hearts, and when we could both breathe without making that squeaking, rattling sound in our throats, we sat up. Nervous eyes scanned the trees and rocks behind us. When neither of us saw any movement, we eased to our feet.

"Where are we?" I whispered.

"Fort Sill," Gary breathed back. "Figure we're about a mile into the grounds. If we keep heading this way, I think—"

"There! See 'em. They're about halfway up that hill!''

Gary and I jumped. We spun. Three men stood near the bottom of the slope. Pointing up, they ran toward us.

We sprinted up the hill—away from the men. We ran as fast and as hard as we could. The slope was so steep that in places we had to run on all fours. Our hands grabbed and clawed at the rock and dirt—our legs churned, driving us higher and higher.

The men hadn't gained on us at all by the time we reached the crest of the hill. But as I topped the ridge and saw what was beyond, I froze in my tracks.

There was a wide valley with nothing but barren rock. There were no trees to hide behind. All I could see was wide-open empty space with not so much as a blade of grass to break the monotony of the rubble.

Then, right in the middle of the emptiness, I saw it!

There was a building. A little shack. Next to it were a couple of trucks. Farther on, a tank—a real army tank. A bright orange, triangular-shaped flag fluttered from a pole on the roof. And there, right beside the front door, two men stood. They wore army helmets and camouflaged uniforms.

Soldiers! They'd help us. They'd save us from the horrible men who were after Gary and me. They'd help Daddy and Patricia.

"Hey!" I screamed. I waved both arms above my head. "Hey! Up here! Help!"

I charged down the hill. The rock was broken and

crunched like gravel under my feet. I picked up more speed with the slope of the hill. I ran—as fast and hard as I had ever run in my life.

"No!" I heard Gary scream behind me.

I ignored him. I guess he hadn't seen the soldiers. He didn't know we were safe. He didn't realize rescue was so near.

Faster and faster I raced down the hill. Suddenly I was going so fast that my feet couldn't keep up. I felt myself lean, my body tilting forward. I tried to make my legs go faster. I lost my balance. When I fell, the gravel tore at my shoulder and back. I didn't let it stop me. I tumbled over once, then again, and popped right back to my feet. I kept running.

Behind me I could hear Gary. He ran. He called my name. I didn't look back. I was on the flat at the bottom of the hill. Only about two hundred more yards to safety. Gary must have seen the shack and the soldiers, too. I could hear his footsteps. They were closer now. He was right behind me—running for the men who would rescue us.

Then there was another sound. It was a whining, whizzing sound, almost like the drone of a low-flying model airplane. The sound was so loud and close, it made me look up.

There was nothing there. I kept running.

The explosion knocked me from my feet. It spun me around and slammed me to the ground. I must have slid at least five yards on my stomach before I stopped.

Frantic, confused, I struggled to my feet. On my right, about as far away as the length of a soccer field, I saw an enormous cloud of dust boiling into the air. Blinking, I looked back at the two soldiers by the little shed. They didn't move. It was like they hadn't heard the explosion. They didn't even turn to look at the dust cloud that swirled higher and higher into the blue sky.

I staggered toward them—a couple of steps—then I was running once more.

The low-pitched drone came to my ears again. The whizzing whining was right above my head.

Another explosion shook the ground beneath my feet. Somehow, I managed to keep my balance. A second dust cloud puffed into the air. This one was farther away than the first—about fifty yards beyond. I ran harder. I had to reach the safety of the little shack. I had to get to the two men and *make* them help us.

Hands caught me from behind. The force yanked me back and to the side so that I lost my balance. My feet flew out from under me and I fell, flat on my back.

Something was on top of me. Someone was holding me down.

Legs kicking and arms shoving against the ground, I tried to get up.

The explosion was so roaring loud, I thought my eardrums were going to burst. Tiny bits of gravel peppered my left leg. I blinked and forced my eyes to open, but a rolling dust cloud swallowed everything from my sight.

All at once someone was pulling me to my feet. Shoving me. It had to be the men. They'd caught us. They were trying to take us back. I had to get away.

I yanked away from the hands and took a step toward the building—toward the soldiers and safety. But I was grabbed again and spun around.

"Help!" I screamed at the top of my lungs. "Help us! Don't let 'em take us!"

Gary stood there. His nose almost touched mine.

"Help!" I shouted again. "Help us."

Gary shook me, hard.

"Shut up and run," he screamed.

I blinked, motioning toward the little shack.

"But the men . . . got to get help . . . got to get there . . ."

Gary shook me again. "No," he roared. "This way. *Run!"*

Another whining, whizzing sound split the air. Then Gary wrapped an arm around my neck and threw both of us to the ground.

No sooner had we hit than another chest-rattling explosion shook us. This one was farther away than the others but still enough to rumble the ground where we lay.

Once more Gary was on his feet, yanking me.

"We're on the range. It's artillery. We gotta get outta here!"

"But ... soldiers ..." I pointed to the shed.

"That's what they're aiming at, you idiot! We gotta go this way."

He tugged me back toward the hill, we had come from. I paused, only a second, to glance at the little building. The two soldiers stood, motionless. They didn't turn, they didn't blink. Their faces were frozen—without expression.

Plastic faces that didn't change. They were mannequins—dummies.

The drone of another artillery shell spiraling through the air whizzed over my head.

CHAPTER 24

"Check your fire! Check your fire!"

The faraway shout made us stop. Shaking, trembling, Gary and I leaned against each other for support. Frantic eyes searched, trying to find where the voice had come from.

"There." Gary pointed.

I followed his finger to a little hill. On a second ridge, beyond the hill where he pointed, I saw a man. This one wore an army helmet and had on a green camouflage shirt and pants—only this man wasn't standing still with a blank plastic stare on his face. The man I saw on the faraway hill was jumping up and down and waving his arms and screaming his head off.

"You blankety-blank idiots," he screeched. "You trying to get yourselves killed? Get out of there! Get up here—*right now*—dumb little . . ." His voice faded into a mumbled scramble of profanity as he kept shaking his fist at us.

Half hidden in a clump of oak trees, I saw a jeep. A man stood in the front seat, one foot on the seat, the other on the dashboard. He held a huge walkie-talkie to his ear and cupped his hand near the mouthpiece.

"Check your fire," he repeated. "Check your fire. Civilians on the range. Looks like a couple of kids. No, sir. I ain't kiddin'. Check your fire!"

The men and the jeep disappeared from our sight as we neared the first hill. The droning sound of shells whizzing above our head stopped. The explosions that rattled my chest and forced us to dive to the ground and cover our heads with our hands stopped, too.

"They're spotters," Gary told me as we started to climb. "Check your fire means he was telling the guys to quit shootin' the howitzers." We kept running, climbing. About halfway up the hill Gary paused to catch his breath. "They're gonna be mad and cussin' us for being out there," he panted. "But they'll help. We're safe now."

When we topped the first hill, we could see the soldier again. He was a young man. His eyes were wide and frantic. When he spotted us coming over the rise, he shook his fist at us once more.

"Get up here! Right now! Lucky you weren't killed. I ought to kill you, myself, you dumb little . . ." Again he spewed profanity at us.

We lost sight of him once more, when we crossed the saddleback ridge between the two hills. As we climbed, working our way up the second hill, I could hear the other man.

"Yes, sir. Smack in the middle of the range. No, sir. Don't look hurt, sir. They're coming up. Yes, sir."

The second hill was steeper than the first. Gary and I were almost crawling by the time we reached the summit. I expected the young soldier to be standing there, waiting for us. I expected him to be yelling and cursing. He was so scared and frantic, it wouldn't have surprised me if he even hit us or slugged us for scaring him so badly. If he hit me, I wouldn't mind.

On our knees, we struggled over the last little lip of rock to get to the top of the hill. We grunted and staggered to our feet. I looked around, wondering where the young soldier had gone and why he wasn't still cursing at us. I frowned when I saw both men sitting in the jeep.

Exhausted, Gary leaned and stumbled toward them. "Don't yell at us no more," he pleaded. "We need help. Just listen . . . you've got to help us . . ."

Neither man looked up. They just sat there. Feet dragging over the ground, I followed Gary toward the jeep.

We were almost there when I saw their eyes. The eyes stared straight ahead. They didn't move. They didn't blink. They were dead, empty eyes—like the lifeless eyes of the mannequins who stood as plastic guards in front of the shed on the target range.

"Post seven?" A voice crackled from the walkie-talkie. "Come back, post seven. Do you have the boys in custody, yet? Corporal Higgins? Answer me, boys. What's goin' on up there? Where are you?"

Another step and I could have reached out and touched the walkie-talkie that lay on the car seat beside the young man. Instead my feet stuck to the ground like they were weighted with cement. The breath caught in my throat.

In that second when I didn't hear my own wheezing and gasping for air, I heard another sound. It was the snap of a twig—a footstep that came from the trees beside me.

I turned.

Benny leaped from his hiding place behind a large oak. In two long, easy strides he closed the distance between us.

"Sorry, kid . . ." His gentle smile seemed almost sad. ". . . but you've caused enough trouble." His steel-gray eyes never blinked.

Before I could scream—before I could even think to run—a huge fist flashed at the corner of my eye. The force slammed against the side of my head like a hammer. It spun me around—spun me farther and farther, until there was nothing but an empty blackness.

CHAPTER 25

*H*ow long the blackness held me, I don't know. Light began to flicker behind my closed eyelids. Like little sparks or flashes of lightning, it urged my eyes to open. I tried to blink. My left eye opened just a crack. My right eye wouldn't budge.

The whole right side of my head throbbed and pulsated with a dull ache. I opened my left eye a bit more, but I still couldn't see. I tried to rub the pain at the right side of my head.

My hands wouldn't move. Something held them behind my back. I pulled and tugged, but it was no use.

" 'Bout time you woke up."

I blinked and turned toward the voice. Gary sat next to me. There was a cut at the side of his mouth. A trail made of dried blood was caked from the cut to the sharp angle at the bottom of his chin. Patricia sat on the floor next to him. Her bare ankles were tied together with nylon stockings. Daddy was on the far side of her, next to the stove. He leaned forward so he could see around Gary and Patricia. He tried to smile.

I looked at Gary.

"How long?" I tried to ask, but my throat and mouth were so dry, the words didn't come out. Gary frowned and leaned his ear closer to me.

"What?"

I mouthed the words again. There was still no sound.

Gary shrugged. "Don't know. It was a little after noon when they caught us. It was dark before I woke up. Figure you been out about seven hours or so."

Other voices came to my ears. They seemed far away and muffled at first, then grew louder and more distinct.

"I don't care what you say. I don't care what Rico says. I been out here nine hours. I'm taking a break."

My left eye fluttered again and finally opened enough so I could see. A short man with thick glasses stood beside an open door, facing me. Even from the back, I could recognize the man he was talking to. He was the one called Benny.

"You only have six more rolls to go," Benny said. "Rico wants it—"

"I don't care what Rico wants," the man with the pop-bottle glasses snapped, interrupting him. "I'm hungry, I'm tired, and I need to take a dump. You and Rico can just wait."

With that, he spun and walked through the open

doorway into the darkness beyond. I tilted my head to the side as my left eye darted about the room.

We were in Daddy's darkroom. I was sitting in a corner with my back against two walls. There were tables, small trays of chemicals, and film—rolls and rolls of film—*everywhere.* Grayish-black strips, held by clothespins, dangled from little wires. Long slices of film, composed of small squares of developed film, lined the floor. The film curled and wound so thick it looked like some weird carpet that covered the ground.

"I was afraid you weren't going to wake up." Benny's feet crunched and crackled through the piles of film that covered the floor as he came toward me. He knelt down, put a hand behind the back of my neck and pulled me forward so he could check the bindings on my hands. "Didn't mean to hit you so hard, kid." His kind smile didn't warm me at all. "You been out awhile. You okay?"

I glared at him.

"Water." The word didn't come out. My tongue stuck against the roof of my mouth.

Benny frowned.

"Water," I repeated.

Benny nodded. He walked over to a table and came back. Gently, he held a glass to my lips and let me drink. The water was warm, but I'd never tasted or felt anything so good as when it trickled down my throat. He put the glass back on the table and started toward the door.

I heard a fluttering sound. It was far away at first, but it grew louder and louder. Benny quickly shut the door and leaned against it.

The fluttering sound changed into a loud puttering. Then—even louder—a popping sound like machine-gun fire, right over our heads. I looked up at the ceiling.

"Helicopter," Gary whispered in my ear. I could barely hear him above the pounding and popping roar. "Army's been out, all over the place, since they killed them two soldiers."

The sound faded as quickly as it had come. When it was quiet, Benny opened the door and peeked out. He sighed and took a step toward the house. Suddenly he stopped. He hesitated a moment, then turned back to us.

Again his feet crunched and crackled through the piles of exposed film when he walked back to where we sat. He checked my hands and then went down the line, checking each of us in turn. When he finished, he knelt in front of Daddy.

"There ain't much time, mister," he said earnestly. "What I'm gonna say is the truth. There ain't no lie to it—so you listen."

Daddy didn't move.

Benny glanced at Patricia, then Gary and me.

"All four of you are already dead," he said flatly. "You just don't know it yet. Now, I don't hold with killing women and children. But the people we work for can't afford to leave any loose ends. So no matter what, all four of you will be dead when we leave here. Do you understand?"

Daddy didn't answer, but when Benny's steel-gray eyes bored into him, Daddy finally gave a tiny nod.

Benny shook his head.

"There's worse things than dying." Benny looked down at the ground and shook his head again. "You and I both know that the film Rico's lookin' for ain't here. There was a total of fifty-eight rolls of film. Mr. Orth has developed fifty-two of them. Ain't nobody that unlucky.

"Now, one way or another, Rico's gonna find that film. If he has to torture you to find out where it is, he will." He leaned toward Daddy and looked at him out of one eye. "Rico's good at that kind of stuff. He likes torturing people. And, you'll talk—*believe me*—you'll talk." He looked at the rest of us once more before he eased to his feet. "Don't let Rico get hold of your wife and the boys," he pleaded. "I swear to you, if I have to do it, it won't hurt. I know how to do it without any hurt—without any pain. But Rico . . . Please, mister, I ain't lying to you . . . don't let him get hold of them."

Daddy only stared at him. After a moment Benny let out a long sigh and headed for the door. Without looking back, he pulled the door shut behind him.

"You ain't got long," he called softly. "Think about what I said."

As soon as the door closed behind him, I shoved my hands and wrists down against the floor. Squirming and wiggling, I began scooting my bound wrists under my seat.

"They take your knife?"

Gary looked at me and frowned.

"Your knife," I repeated. "You still got it?"

Gary nodded. I pushed harder. Fingers wiggling, shifting my weight back and forth—first one side and then the other—I moved my wrists under my bottom. My butt clunked against the cement floor when my hands slipped from under it to the bend of my knees.

Leaning forward, I pushed my face and head between my knees. The nylon stockings that held my wrists were tight. I guess the men had taken our shoes, just in case Gary and I managed to get free and try to run again. It was a good thing they had because if I'd had my shoes on, I don't think I could have gotten my wrists past my feet.

Once I'd pulled my hips and legs through the loop made by my arms and had my hands in front of me, I got to my knees and crawled to Gary.

"Left pocket," he whispered.

I dug around until I found his pocketknife. I pulled the blade out and, using my forehead, shoved Gary over on his side so I could reach the stockings that held his hands. The knife was sharp. I sawed through the nylon in the blink of an eye. Gary grabbed the knife from me and cut his legs loose. Then he released me.

After handing the knife back, he scampered over to watch at the door while I got Daddy and Patricia free.

"What do we do now?" Gary whispered from across the room.

Daddy shook his head. "I don't know. They brought in two more carloads of men. I think there's nine of 'em, counting that Orth guy who's been developing and tearin' up all the film. There's too many. We can't fight 'em. If we ran, they'd just catch us . . . and . . . I don't know what to do."

"If there was just some way we could signal." Patricia rubbed her wrists and looked around. "With all the helicopters flying over. A fire. Something. Some way to get their attention."

Gary grabbed the BB gun from next to the door and brought it over.

"On the cliff," he said. "There's a little overhang off to the right. Kinda like a little cave, sort of. It's not very deep, but all four of us could squeeze into it. They can't see us from up here. We could hide there until daylight, then maybe a helicopter would spot us or—"

Daddy pointed to the BB gun in his hand. "What are you doin' with that? What's—"

Gary flipped the gun upside down. I heard the little BBs rattle as they rolled down the barrel. Once he had it turned, he began unscrewing a little knob in the center of the butt.

"The holder thing," Gary explained. "In the butt of the BB gun. It's big enough to hold three packs of BBs. When I heard what was going on in the house, I came out here and hid the film." He removed the knob and tipped the gun. A roll of film slipped out into his hand. He gave it to Daddy. "I hid this roll of film in the BB gun before I dumped the rest of it out on the floor."

Daddy stuffed the film in his pocket and quietly slipped over to the back door.

"Hurry," he urged. "We'll hide where Gary said."

Patricia followed him. Gary dropped the BB gun and trotted after them.

"Come on, Sam."

I stood, staring at the BB gun.

"Sam?" Gary repeated.

I stared at the stove—the one that Daddy said leaked. I remembered the stench of butane that gave me a headache the night we developed my film.

"Hurry, Sam," Daddy's shouted whisper was urgent and scared.

I remembered what Patricia had said: *If there was just some way to signal* . . . And I remembered Justin Porter, my friend back in Connecticut.

"Now!" Gary growled. "Before somebody comes."

I grabbed the BB gun and chased after my family.

CHAPTER 26

It was a good fifteen minutes—plenty of time—before the man with the thick glasses came back from the house. I stood on the lip of rock just over the edge of the cliff. On my tiptoes, I could barely see over the ledge.

Gary stood beside me. Some twenty feet from where we hid, where the ledge narrowed, was a shallow overhang in the rock. Daddy had pushed Patricia into it and lay, holding her. It took some effort, but I had finally convinced him that I knew what I was doing.

It took a little more convincing with Gary.

"Here he comes," Gary whispered. "You sure about this."

I shook my head. "No," I confessed. "It only works in old model BB guns. This one's old. But I'm not sure.

"What if it's not old enough?" Gary said. "What if it don't work?"

I shrugged, then shushed him when I saw the little man with the thick glasses waddle across the yard. At the front of the shack he disappeared from my view when he opened the door. He started coughing. In a second he appeared again. He was bent over, holding his chest and fanning his face.

After he coughed and gagged and coughed some more, he finally caught his breath. When he did, he straightened up, looked toward the house and cupped his hands around his mouth like a megaphone.

"Rico! Benny!" he called. "Get out here. They're gone!"

The back door burst open. Five men trotted from the house, so close together that they kept bumping against one another. About halfway across the yard they stopped.

"What did you say?" I recognized Rico's sleazy voice.

"They're gone," the man with the glasses repeated. "All four of them are gone."

The group of men rushed on. Others joined them from the house—a whole mob trotted across the backyard toward us.

Rico, in the lead, stopped right in front of the little man with the thick glasses. When he stopped, so did the others behind him.

"What do you mean, gone?" he demanded.

"Just like I said. They're gone. All four."

Rico spun around. He slapped Benny across the face.

"I told you to check. Not to leave them unless you were sure they couldn't get loose."

"I did check." Benny's voice was smooth, and warm as honey dripping from a tree. "And, Rico . . ."

"What?"

"You ever touch me again, I'll kill you." The smooth, relaxed flow of his voice never changed.

Rico spun back toward Daddy's darkroom. The others followed. All but the little man with thick glasses disappeared at the front of the shack.

"All four of 'em are gone," he repeated. "Ratcliff, don't go in there with that cigarette. There's a gas leak or somethin'."

The plastic stock of the BB gun felt cold against my cheek. The hinge on the front door made a squeaking sound.

"A gas leak?" Rico asked.

"Yeah. And . . ."

I aimed at the cement floor where we had left the back door cracked. Rico coughed. So did some of the others.

I squeezed the trigger.

A little twang came from the spring. The kitchen match that I'd taken from Gary's match holder went "poof" as it flew from the barrel.

The instant I shot, I closed my eyes. Still, it wasn't quick enough. The match struck the cement floor. A little yellow-blue flame ignited.

The explosion from the butane gas was blue, then yellow, then white-hot. Even with my eyes closed, it almost blinded me.

I dropped the gun. Gary and I ducked behind the cliff.

The explosion was deafening.

Even sheltered behind the solid rock cliff, the roar and the sound waves that rushed before it almost shook us from the narrow ledge. We clung to one another. We grabbed at the bare rock.

The roar seemed to last and last. Beside us we could see bits of flaming wood floating down into the canyon below. On our hands and knees we crawled to where Daddy and Patricia hid in the tiny cave. We crowded in beside them and watched as more wood and sparks and flames sprayed over our heads to plummet into the canyon like a red and yellow waterfall cascading down a cliff.

It took only moments for the first helicopter to get there. Above the popping, puttering of the motor, we heard the crackling hiss as the barn caught fire. A second helicopter arrived. Spotlights danced across the face of the cliff where we hid, then left as they circled above the house. After a while there was another explosion.

"Gas tank on one of their cars," Daddy said.

That explosion was followed by a second and then a third. Another helicopter came.

It wasn't until we heard the sirens from the rural

fire department that we finally climbed from our hiding place.

Dazed, shaken, and hurt, we staggered into the midst of the fire trucks and the helicopters and the military personnel who had begun to arrive. We walked into the center of all that confusion, and for the first time in three days we felt safe and relaxed.

CHAPTER 27

For the rest of that evening and for the two days that followed, Daddy, Patricia, Gary, and I were guests of the United States Army.

They put us in the helicopters. I'd never been in a helicopter before. It was neat. They flew us back to Fort Sill for what they called "debriefing." What that meant is we stayed up all night answering one question after another. Doctors and nurses came. They checked Patricia, took care of Gary's cut at the corner of his mouth, checked my black eye and wrapped the blisters on my heels. After they checked us over and made sure we were okay, they fed us and we got to answer more questions. It was almost morning before they let us get some sleep. That afternoon they woke us up and we got "debriefed" some more.

About mid-morning of the second day, Mother and Randall arrived. The military had flown them to Oklahoma. Mother hugged and kissed me until I thought my eyes were going to pop out. Randall even hugged me, which really wasn't like him.

At first I didn't know if they had brought Mama and Randall because they were worried about me or if they just wanted to ask them questions, too. After talking for a few moments and finding out that they'd stayed up all night on their flight and answered questions, I knew.

We only got to visit for a short time before some men in uniform came. They put us in cars and drove all six of us across Fort Sill to a big concrete block building.

Two men greeted us in a small room at the back of the place. A plump, jovial man with a broad smile stood in the doorway, shook hands with each of us, and motioned us to come in.

"I'm Nathanial Syzemore." He grinned. "I'm the assistant director of the Federal Bureau of Investigation. This—" He stepped aside so we could see the short man behind him. The man had the kind of face you could look at and a minute later not remember. "—this is Carl Parks. He's assistant deputy director of the Central Intelligence Agency."

There were eight chairs in the little room facing a white screen. Beside one of the chairs was a slide projector.

"Normally, we don't let the public in on matters of national security," Mr. Syzemore said as he sat in the chair beside the projector. He cleared his throat. "But after everything you and your family have been through, and because of the impending cover-up that we feel is necessary for your safety and that of your family, we feel that full disclosure is in order."

Gary sat in the chair next to me. He leaned over and nudged me with his elbow.

"What the heck did he say?"

"They're gonna tell us what's goin' on," I answered.

A picture appeared on the white screen. Mr. Syzemore snapped his fingers and the lights went out. On the screen were two Learjets. A group of men stood around in front of them.

"That's the picture," I yelped. "That's the picture I took at the airport."

Mr. Syzemore almost laughed. "That's right, Sam. That's what all this fuss was about."

"That's Rico." Gary pointed to the dark-complected man in the center of the picture. "And there's Ratcliff and Tubby and Benny."

"The men you recognize," Mr. Syzemore said, "are mercenaries." He cleared his throat and glanced at Gary and me. "They're professional killers. If you boys hadn't blown up that shed—which, by the way, was one of the most ingenious maneuvers I've ever heard of—anyway, if you hadn't, these guys would have killed you. There's no doubt in my mind, and they wouldn't have thought twice about it."

He clicked the projector and the same picture appeared again, only this time it looked a little bigger and closer. "The man on the right, in the Panama hat, is Pablo Senario. In our line of work, he's what's called a 'provider.' He works with drug kingpins, terrorist groups, anyone who has enough money. If they're willing to pay, Pablo Senario will provide whatever they need. Anything from rare art to weapons, explosives, drugs. You name it and have the money to pay for it—Pablo Senario provides it for you. The man in the derby hat," he continued, "is Daniel Carington. Mr. Carington is a United States senator. Either the chairman or a member of a number of influential committees, he has a very high security clearance, and—"

"And," Daddy cut him off, kind of explaining to Gary and me both, "if this picture ever got to the press, with a big-shot senator hanging around with a bunch of crooks, the guy's political carer would be finished."

Mr. Syzemore cleared his throat. "There's more to it, Mr. Ross." He clicked the button on the projector and the next slide appeared. "We had to use computer enhancements and laser adaptations to magnify some of these prints, but I think after you see them, you'll understand."

Pictures began to flash on the screen. First there was a close-up of Benny. The next picture showed a newspaper under his arm. Finally, a really close-up shot of the date on the paper. It was the day I left Connecticut to come to Oklahoma.

There was a picture of Senator Carington. He was unrolling a piece of yellowish-brown canvas. In succession, each picture got closer and closer, until we could see some number on the back of the canvas: REM-10017.

"That is the identification number of a painting stolen from a museum in Rome, Italy, over a year ago. It's a most valuable piece of art. The last time it was sold at auction was twenty-eight years ago, and it went for over 1.8 million dollars. With the aide of this photograph, we were able to obtain a federal search warrant. The painting was found in a safe in Senator Carington's home."

Pictures of Pablo Senario appeared. The close-ups kept going and going until they got to a tiny object he held between his thumb and finger.

"I bet it's a diamond," Gary whispered in my ear.

"Nope," Mr. Parks, the pudgy guy from the Central Intelligence Agency who sat on the other side of Mr. Syzemore, whispered back.

Another picture clicked and I could make out some letters and numbers. Mostly, the picture was fuzzy—only dots that I had to squint to see.

"T-CU2307P-4," Mr. Parks said softly, "is a computer chip. I can't tell you much about it, only that it's part of the guidance system for the newest, most accurate surface-to-air missile in the world. If this guidance chip fell into the wrong hands . . . as it did . . ." He sighed and shook his head. Then he smiled. "Our agents caught Pablo Senario boarding a plane in Mexico City for . . . well, it's what we call 'a less than friendly' country. The Mexican authorities were very cooperative in sending him back to the States."

The lights came on. We all blinked and covered our eyes. Mr. Parks cleared his throat and looked around at Mr. Syzemore and at us.

"Bottom line is that on the evening news, there will be special coverage of Senator Carington and Pablo Senario being taken into custody by federal agents. The pictures that Sam took will be shown, but we're telling the press that they were taken by one of our agents." He looked at me and shrugged. "This should keep Sam out of it. Just to be on the safe side—with your permission—we have assigned agents to keep both families under constant surveillance until the trial is over."

Randall and Daddy both agreed. After they signed some papers about having people watch us and even having what they called "taps" put on our phones, we left for the airport.

While the grown-ups said their good-byes and thank-yous, Gary and I slipped over in the corner.

"The Wichitas are really fun," he said. "Lots of things I'd like to show you. There's a neat place to swim, and a waterfall. All sorts of stuff, if you got time to look at it, 'stead of running through it like we had to this time."

"I think you ought to come to Connecticut next summer," I suggested.

Gary frowned. "Don't sound like there's much to do there. Shopping malls and video games. Not much excitement."

I laughed. "Well, not as much as we had here, I hope."

"Me, too." He rolled his eyes and we both laughed.

When Mother and Randall started down the ramp to board the plane, I stopped at the doorway. Daddy hugged me and kissed me good-bye. Patricia kissed me, too. Gary shook his head.

"I ain't gonna kiss ya," he said with a smirk. "You too ugly." So we shook hands and I walked after Mother and Randall.

About halfway down the ramp I stopped. I felt a grin on my face. It was one of those sloppy grins— the kind Gary used on me. I felt my tongue trace a little circle around the inside of my mouth when I turned to look back at him.

"Reckon you might oughta fetch some Sunday-go-to-meetin' clothes when you come," I called. "Ain't no sense bein' underdressed when you come to Connecticut."

Gary smiled back and shook his head.

As the plane finally pulled away from the terminal and taxied toward the runway, I could see Daddy and Patricia and Gary waving as we moved away. I pressed my face close to the glass and waved back.

I never had a brother before. I never really wanted one. Now, I was glad I did.

I was glad I had Gary.

ABOUT THE AUTHOR

When BILL WALLACE was a child, his family had a summer cottage in the Wichita Mountains. Bill was a principal and physical education teacher at the same elementary school he attended as a child in his hometown of Chickasha, Oklahoma, for ten years. He and his family still enjoy spending their spare time exploring in the mountains.

Bill and his family have four dogs, three cats, and two horses. He lectures at schools around the country, answers mail from his readers, and of course, works on his books. His novels have won sixteen state awards and made the master lists in twenty-four states.